SCHOLASTIQUE
MUKASONGA

Our Lady
of the Nile

Translated from the French
by Melanie Mauthner

archipelago books

First published as *Notre-Dame du Nil* by Éditions Gallimard, Paris, 2012.

Library of Congress Cataloging-in-Publication Data
Mukasonga, Scholastique.
Our Lady of the Nile / Scholastique Mukasonga ; translated from the
French by Melanie Mauthner.
pages cm
ISBN 978-0-914671-03-9
1. Girls – Education – Rwanda – Fiction. 2. Rwanda – Social conditions – Fiction.
3. Rwanda – Politics and government – 1962-1994 – Fiction.
I. Mauthner, Melanie L., 1964- translator. II. Title.
PQ3989.3.M843N6813 2014
843'.92 – dc23   2014024136

Archipelago Books
232 Third Street #A111
Brooklyn, NY 11215
www.archipelagobooks.org

Distributed by Random House
www.randomhouse.com

Cover art: Amedeo Modigliani
Book design by David Bullen

With immense thanks to Roland Glasser

Archipelago Books is grateful for the generous support of the Lannan Foundation,
the National Endowment for the Arts, the New York City Department of
Cultural Affairs, and the New York State Council on the Arts, a state agency.

This work, published as part of a program providing publication assistance,
received financial support from the French Ministry of Foreign Affairs,
the Cultural Services of the French Embassy in the United States,
and FACE (French American Cultural Exchange).

PRINTED IN THE UNITED STATES OF AMERICA

Our Lady

of the Nile

Our Lady
of the Nile

There is no better lycée than Our Lady of the Nile. Nor is there any higher. Twenty-five hundred meters, the white teachers proudly proclaim. "Two thousand four hundred ninety-three meters," points out Sister Lydwine, our geography teacher. "We're so close to heaven," whispers Mother Superior, clasping her hands together.

The school year coincides with the rainy season, so the lycée is often wrapped in clouds. Sometimes, not often, the sun peaks through and you can see as far as the big lake, that shiny blue puddle down in the valley.

It's a girls' lycée. The boys stay down in the capital. The reason for building the lycée so high up was to protect the girls, by keeping them far away from the temptations and evils of the big city. Good marriages await these young lycée ladies, you see. And they must be virgins when they wed – or at least not get pregnant beforehand. Staying a virgin is better, for marriage is a serious business. The lycée's boarders are daughters of ministers, high-ranking army officers, businessmen, and rich merchants. Their daughters' weddings are the stuff of politics, and the girls are proud of this – they know what they're worth. Gone are the days when beauty was all that mattered. Their families will receive far more than cattle or the traditional jugs of beer for their dowry, they'll get suitcases stuffed full of banknotes, or a healthy account with the Banque Belgolaise in Nairobi or Brussels. Thanks to their daughters, these families will grow wealthy, the power of their clans will be strengthened, and the influence of their lineage will spread far and wide. The young ladies of Our Lady of the Nile know just how much they are worth.

The lycée is very close to the Nile, to its source, in fact. To get there, you follow a rocky trail along the ridgeline. It leads to a flat parking area for the few tourist Land Rovers venturing that far. A sign reads: SOURCE OF THE NILE ➔ 200 M. A steep path brings you to a heap of rocks where the rivulet spurts between two stones. The water pools in a cement basin, then dribbles over in a thin cascade and along a little channel, before disappearing down the grassy hillside into the tree ferns of the valley. To the right, a pyramid has been erected, bearing the inscription: SOURCE OF THE NILE. COCK MISSION, 1924. It's not a very tall pyramid: the girls from the lycée can easily touch the broken tip – they say it brings good luck. Yet it's not the pyramid that draws them to the source. They're not here to explore; they're on a pilgrimage. The statue of Our Lady of the Nile looms among the large rocks overhanging the spring. It's not quite a grotto, although a sheet-metal shelter protects her from the elements. OUR LADY OF THE NILE, 1953, reads the engraved pedestal. It was Monsignor the Vicar Apostolic who decided to erect the statue, in order to consecrate the Nile to the Virgin Mary, despite the King of Belgium persuading the Sovereign Pontiff to consecrate the whole country to Christ the King.

Some people still remember the unveiling ceremony. Sister Kizito, the old, somewhat frail cook, was there that day. Every year she describes the occasion to the new pupils. "Oh, it was a beautiful ceremony, similar to those you see in church, in Kigali, at Christmas, or in the stadium, on Rwanda's National Day.

"The King's official representative sent an envoy, but the colonial administrator was there too, flanked by an escort of ten soldiers. One held a bugle, another carried the Belgian flag. Various chiefs and deputy chiefs were in attendance, along with those from neighboring chiefdoms. They brought their wives and daughters, who wore their hair piled high and pinned with pearls, they brought their dancers, who shook their manes like valiant lions,

9

and of course they brought their herds of long-horned *inyambo* cattle decked with flower garlands. The hillside was thronged with farmers. Naturally, the whites from the capital didn't dare venture onto the rough path that led to the spring. But Monsieur de Fontenaille, the coffee planter who lived next door to the lycée, was there, sitting beside the administrator. It was the dry season. The sky was clear. No haze wreathed the mountain peaks.

"We waited. Finally, a black line could be seen approaching on the ridge path, and a murmur of hymns and prayers arose. One by one they came into focus: Monsignor the Vicar Apostolic, with his miter and crosier, looking like one of the Three Wise Men from the pictures they show in catechism class. The missionaries walked behind him: they wore pith helmets, as all the whites did back then, but were bearded and dressed in long white robes with a chunky rosary around their necks. Children from the Legion of Mary strewed the path with yellow petals. Then came the Virgin. Four seminary boys in shorts and white shirts carried her on a plaited-bamboo litter, the kind used to take a young bride to her new family, or the dead to their final resting place. But it was impossible to see the Madonna because she was wrapped in a blue and white veil. Behind her jostled the 'native clergy,' and then, preceded by their banner and the white and yellow papal flag, came the straggling line of catechism pupils, straying cheerfully off the path onto the slopes, despite the best efforts of the monitors with their sticks.

"The procession reached the hollow and the spring; the Madonna's palanquin was lowered beside the stream – she was still hidden beneath the veil. The administrator stepped forward and greeted Monsignor with a military salute, exchanging a few words while the rest of the procession took up position around the spring and the statue, which had been raised onto a little stage. The Bishop climbed the five steps with two missionaries, blessed the crowd, then turned to face the statue and recited an oration in Latin, with the two priests giving the response. Suddenly, with a nod and a wave from the Bishop, one of the acolytes unveiled the Madonna. The bugle sounded, the flag was dipped, and a hushed murmur spread through the crowd. The hollow filled with the women's sharp cries of joy and the jingling of the dancers' ankle bells. The Virgin who appeared from beneath the veil certainly resembled Our Lady of Lourdes, who can be seen at the mission church dressed in the same blue veil, the same azure belt, the same yellow dress, but Our Lady of the Nile was black: her face was black, her hands were black, her feet were black. Our Lady of the Nile was a black woman, an African woman, a Rwandan woman – and indeed, why not?

"'It's Isis,' cried Monsieur de Fontenaille. 'She has returned!'

"And so, with a vigorous sprinkling of holy water, Monsignor the Vicar Apostolic blessed the statue, blessed the spring, and blessed the crowd. Then he delivered his sermon. Not all of what he said was comprehensible. He spoke of the Holy Virgin, and how she would be known here as Our Lady of the Nile. He said: 'The drops of this holy water shall mix with the burgeoning waters of the Nile, which in turn shall mix with other streams and become The River, flowing through lakes, flowing through swamps, pouring over waterfalls, braving the desert sands, soaking the cells of bygone monks, even lapping at the feet of the surprised Sphinx. It is as if, by the grace of Our Lady of the Nile, these holy drops were to baptize all of Africa; and Africa – now Christian – shall save this world from perdition. And I see, yes, I see, crowds thronging here from all the nations in pilgrimage, yes, in pilgrimage, to our mountains, to give grace to Our Lady of the Nile.'"

When his turn came, Chief Kayitare walked up to the stage and called to Rutamu, his cow, which he offered to the new Queen of Rwanda. He praised both the cow and the Virgin Mary, saying they would provide milk and honey in abundance. The women's cries of joy and the tinkle of the dancers' bells approved this auspicious gift.

A few days later, workers from the mission arrived to erect a platform between the two colossal rocks overhanging the spring. They placed the statue on it, beneath a shelter of sheet metal. It was much later that they built the lycée, two kilometers away, just as Rwanda gained independence.

Perhaps Monsignor hoped that the spring's holy water would prove to be as miraculous as that of Lourdes. Alas no. There is only Kagabo the healer – or poisoner – who fills small black jugs shaped like a calabash with water from the spring. In these he soaks scary-looking roots, sloughed-off snake skins crushed into powder, tufts of hair from stillborns, and the dried blood from girls' first menstruations. Concoctions to heal, or to kill, it depends.

For a long time, the photos of the unveiling ceremony of Our Lady of the Nile lined the long corridor where visitors, or parents who had requested a meeting with Mother Superior, were asked to wait. Now there was only one photograph still hanging: the one with Monsignor the Vicar Apostolic blessing the statue. Only traces of the others remained, the slightly paler marks of rectangular frames on the wall, there behind the hard wooden sofa – no cushion in sight – on which the unfortunate pupils summoned by the fearsome Mother Superior never dared to sit. Yet the photos hadn't been destroyed. Gloriosa, Modesta, and Veronica found them one day when they were asked to clean the room at the back of the library where the archives were stacked. There, under a heap of old newspapers and magazines (*Kinyamateka*, *Kurerera Imana*, *L'Ami*, *Grands Lacs*, etc.), they found the photos, slightly discolored and warped, some still covered by a sheet of broken glass. There was the photo of the administrator making his military salute before the statue, and the soldier behind him dipping the Belgian flag. There were the photos of the *intore* dancers – slightly blurred because the inept photographer tried to capture their impressive leaps in midair, which caused their sisal manes and leopard skins to be wreathed in a ghostly halo. Then there was the photo of the chiefs and their wives in all their finery, but most of these dignitaries had been crossed through with a wide stroke of red ink, and the faces of others masked by a question mark in black.

"The chiefs' photos have suffered the *social revolution*," said Gloriosa, laughing. "A dash of ink, a slash of machete, that's all it takes . . . and no more Tutsi."

"What about the ones with a question mark?" Modesta wanted to know.

"Alas, they must be the ones who managed to flee! But now that they're in Bujumbura or Kampala, those big chiefs have lost their cattle, and their pride. They drink water like the pariahs they've become. I'm taking the photos. My father will tell me who these whip masters are."

Veronica wondered when she, too, would be crossed out with red ink, on the annual class photograph taken at the start of the school year.

The pupils of Our Lady of the Nile make their great pilgrimage in May, the Virgin Mary's month. Pilgrimage day is a long and beautiful one, and the lycée spends many months preparing for it. Prayers are given for good weather. Mother Superior and Father Herménégilde, the chaplain, announce a novena and request that every class relay each other in the chapel to ask the Holy Virgin to chase off the clouds on that given day! After all, it's quite possible in May: the rains become less frequent as the dry season approaches. For a whole month now, Brother Auxile has been rehearsing the hymns he's written in honor of Our Lady of the Nile. Brother Auxile is the resident handyman, peering into the oily entrails of the electric generator, or the engines of the two supply trucks, cursing the drivers, and the servant-mechanics, in his Ghent dialect. He plays the harmonium and conducts the choir. The Belgian teachers were urged to take part in the ceremony, as were the three young Frenchmen posted here in lieu of military service. Mother Superior hinted, gently but firmly, that as it was a solemn occasion, they should wear a jacket and tie, instead of those ugly trousers they call blue jeans, and that she was counting on them to behave respectfully and set an example for the pupils. Sister Bursar spent a good part of the night in the pantry, setting aside items for the picnic: corned beef, sardines in oil, jam, Kraft cheese. You could hear the jangle of the huge bunch of keys attached to her leather belt. She counted out just enough crates of Fanta for the pupils, and a few bottles of Primus lager for the chaplain, Brother Auxile, and Father Angelo from the nearby mission. For the Rwandan Sisters, the teachers, and the school monitors, she put aside a demijohn of pineapple wine, the specialty of Sister Kizito, who jealously guards the secret recipe.

Of course Mass is endless that day, with hymns, prayers, and dozens of rosary recitations, but best of all is the wild laughter of the girls as they race and romp about, sliding down the grassy slope. Sister Angélique and Sister Rita, the school monitors, blow the hell out of their whistles, bellowing: "Watch out for the ravine!"

Mats are laid down for the picnic. It's not like in the refectory, it's more chaotic, everyone can sit however they like, they can squat down or stretch out, their mouths smeared with jam. The school monitors raise their arms to the sky in defeat. Mother Superior, Sister Gertrude (Mother Superior's Rwandan deputy), Sister Bursar, Father Herménégilde, and Father Angelo all sit on folding chairs. The teachers are also allowed chairs, but the French teachers prefer to sit on the grass. Sister Rita serves the men beer – only a Rwandan woman could have such good manners. Mother Superior of course refuses the Primus she's offered, and Sister Bursar reluctantly does the same, making do with some of Sister Kizito's pineapple wine.

It's rare to see an actual pilgrim mingling with the pupils, since Mother Superior aims to keep at bay any unwelcome guests who might, on a "devotional" pretext, be drawn by the sight of such a gathering of young girls. The mayor of Nyaminombe district, where the lycée is located, has prohibited access to the spring at Mother Superior's request. Even the government minister's wife, who invited a few girlfriends along in her Mercedes to dote on their pious daughters, has a hard time persuading the police officer to lift the barrier. But there's one visitor Mother Superior can't keep away, and that's Monsieur de Fontenaille, the coffee grower. The girls are a bit scared of him. People say he lives alone in his large dilapidated villa. Most of his coffee bushes are going to seed. Nobody knows if he's deranged or a white witch doctor as he goes about organizing digs to search for bones and skulls. His old jeep ignores the paths, jolting up and down the mountain slopes. He always breezes in, mid-picnic, sweeping off his bush hat in a theatrical gesture to greet Mother Superior, exposing his shaven head: "Please accept my deepest respects, Reverend Mother."

She struggles to hide her annoyance: "Good day, Monsieur de Fontenaille, we weren't expecting you. Please, don't intrude on our pilgrimage."

"Like you, I'm here to honor our Mother of the Nile," he replies while turning his back to her. Slowly, he circles each mat where the girls are eating their lunches, stops near one of them, unconsciously adjusts his glasses, searches her face while nodding, pleased with himself, and begins to sketch her profile in his notebook. She'll lower her gaze, as well-brought-up girls do, to avoid his piercing stare, then look away, yet some of the girls can't help slipping him a sly smile. Mother Superior doesn't dare intervene, for fear of causing an even greater scandal, but she follows the old plantation owner's movements with apprehension. At last, he trundles to the little pool brimming with water from the spring, takes a handful of scarlet petals from one of his many jacket pockets, and throws them into the headwaters of the Nile. Then he raises his arms to the sky three times, palms spread, arms wide, and mumbles some incomprehensible incantation. As soon as Monsieur de Fontenaille returns to the parking lot and we hear his jeep begin to stutter, Mother Superior stands and declares: "Come, young ladies, let's sing a hymn." The girls sing in unison, some of them gazing wistfully at the dust trail from the retreating jeep.

Upon returning to the lycée, Veronica opens up her geography book. It's quite tricky to follow the course of the Nile, she has no name to start off with and then there are too many. She seems to have multiple sources, she hides in a lake, resurfaces, turns white, then gets lost in a swamp, while her Blue brother appears somewhere else. She's easier to keep track of near the end, where she flows in a straight line, with desert on either side, lapping at the foot of the pyramids – the big ones – before spreading chaotically into the delta, and finally gushing into the sea, which is far bigger than the lake, so they say.

Veronica realizes that someone is peering over her shoulder, staring at the open page of the textbook with her.

"So, are you looking for the way back to where your people came from, Veronica? Don't worry, I'll pray to Our Lady of the Nile that the crocodiles carry you there on their backs, or rather in their bellies."

Veronica would be forever haunted by Gloriosa's laugh, especially in her nightmares.

Back to School

Our Lady of the Nile: how proudly the school stands. The track leading to the lycée from the capital, winds its interminable way through a labyrinth of hills and valleys and ends, quite unexpectedly, in a twisting climb up the Ikibira Mountains – which geography textbooks call the Congo-Nile range, for want of any other name. The lycée's imposing main building comes into view, and it almost feels as if the peaks have eased themselves aside to make room for the school, there on the edge of the opposite slope, at the bottom of which you glimpse the sparkling lake. The lycée sits on the mountaintop, glinting at the schoolgirls, a palace that shines with their impossible dreams.

The construction of the lycée was a spectacle that Nyaminombe won't forget in a long time. Not wishing to miss a thing, the normally idle men abandoned their jugs of beer in the bar, the women left their fields of millet and peas earlier than usual, and at the sound of the beating drum that announced the end of class, the mission-school children ran out and scrambled through the small crowd watching and commenting on the work in progress, to be in the front row. The more intrepid pupils had already slipped out of school to line the track, watching for the dust cloud that would announce the arrival of the trucks. As soon as the convoy reached them, they ran behind the vehicles and tried to grab hold. Some succeeded, others fell off and barely missed getting run over by the next truck. The drivers hollered in vain, trying to shoo away the swarm of daredevil kids. Some stopped their vehicles and stepped down, and the kids would scamper off, with the driver pretending to chase them, but as soon as the truck started off again, the game began anew. The women in the fields lifted their hoes to the heavens in a gesture of powerlessness and desperation.

Everyone was amazed to see no smoking pyramids of baking bricks, no procession of farmers carrying bricks on their heads, as they did when the *umupadri* asked the faithful to build a new church annex or when the mayor summoned the local people on a Saturday to help with community projects, such as enlarging the clinic or his house. No, this was a real white man's construction site in Nyaminombe, with real white laborers, fearsome iron-jawed machines that ripped and gouged the earth, trucks carrying machines that made an infernal racket and spewed cement, foremen barking orders in Swahili at the masons, and even white overseers who did nothing but look at large sheets of paper they unrolled like bolts of cloth from the Pakistani shop, and who went crazy with rage when they called the black foremen over, as if they were breathing fire.

Of all the lore surrounding the construction site, the most memorable is the story of Gakere. The Gakere Affair. People still recount it today, and it always raises a laugh. The end of each month was payday in Nyaminombe – the thirtieth, a perilous day. Perilous for bookkeepers, subjected to the workers' often violent complaints. Perilous for the day laborers who knew that the thirtieth was the only date their wives remembered: they'd not be in the fields but waiting in the doorway of the hut to take the banknotes their husband handed them; they'd check the amount, tie a piece of banana fiber around the paltry wad, slip it into a little jug, and hide it under the straw by the bedside table. The thirtieth was marked by all kinds of quarrels and violence.

Tables for the bookkeepers were set up beneath awnings, or under shelters made from straw and bamboo. Gakere was a bookkeeper, and it was he who paid the day laborers. He was a former deputy chief of Nyaminombe, who had been purged like so many others by the colonial authorities and replaced by another deputy chief (soon to be mayor), who was a Hutu. Gakere was hired because he knew everyone, all the local hired hands who didn't speak Swahili. Bookkeepers from the capital were hired to pay the others, the real builders, who'd come from elsewhere and did speak Swahili. Everyone queued at the bookkeepers' tables – come rain (usually) or shine – and there was always shouting and shoving, complaints, arguments, and recriminations. The heavies who guarded the construction site kept order, whacking the recalcitrant workers into submission with their sticks – the mayor and his two gendarmes didn't want to get involved, neither did the whites. So Gakere settled beneath his shelter with his cash box under his arm. He sat down, placed the little box on the table, and opened it. The cash box was full of banknotes. Slowly, he unfolded the sheet of paper, a list of names of all the workers he had to pay, workers who'd waited hours. He began the roll call: Bizimana, Habineza . . . The laborer approached the table. Gakere pushed the few notes and coins owed toward him, the laborer pressed an ink-blackened finger next to his name, and Gakere muttered a few words to him as he marked the list with a cross. So for an entire day, Gakere was again the chief he had once been.

Then, one payday he didn't show up: no Gakere, no cash box. It was soon known that he'd run off with the little box stuffed full of notes. "He's gone to Burundi," people said. "Crafty Gakere, he's fled with the Bazungu's money, but how will we get paid now?" Gakere was both admired and condemned: "He shouldn't have taken the money intended for the people of Nyaminombe, he could have figured out how to take the money from somewhere else." But, in the end, the day laborers did get paid, people stopped begrudging Gakere, and no more was heard of him for two months. He'd abandoned his wife and his daughters, who were questioned by the mayor and closely watched by the gendarmes. But Gakere hadn't told them of his dishonest plans: rumor had it that he planned to use the money to take a new wife in Burundi, a younger, prettier one. And then he returned to Nyaminombe, hands tied behind his back, two soldiers escorting him. He had never reached Burundi. He'd been afraid to cross Nyungwe Forest, because of the leopards, the big monkeys, and even the elephants who hadn't roamed the forest for years. He'd traveled the entire country with that little cash box under his arm. He'd tried to cross the large swamps in Bugesera, and lost his way. Burundi wasn't far but he'd wandered in circles through the stands of papyrus sedge, without ever reaching the border, which, it's true, wasn't marked. They eventually found him, on the edge of the swamp, thin and exhausted, his legs swollen. The banknotes were nothing but a spongy mass floating in his water-filled cash box. They tied him to a post by the site entrance for a whole day, to serve as an example. The workers filing past didn't curse or spit at him, just lowered their heads and pretended not to notice. His wife and his two daughters sat at his feet. One of them would get up from time to time, wipe his face and give him a drink. Gakere was convicted but didn't stay in prison very long. He was never seen in Nyaminombe again. It could be that he reached Burundi at last with his wife and daughters, but without his little box. Some wondered whether the Bazungu had cast a spell on the banknotes, whether those wretched notes had made poor Gakere spin like a top, and that was why he never managed to reach Burundi.

The lycée is a large four-story building, higher than the government ministries in the capital. When the new girls first arrive, the ones from the countryside are afraid to get too close to the windows in the fourth-floor dorms. "Are we going to sleep perched like little monkeys?" they ask. The town girls, and the veterans, tease the new arrivals, pushing them toward the windows: "Look down there," they say. "You're going to fall into the lake!" Eventually, the new girls get used to it. The chapel, nearly as high as the mission church, is also made of cement, but the gym, bursar's office, workshops, and Brother Auxile's garage are all made of brick. They form a courtyard closed off by a wall, with a metal gate that whines when it's opened in the morning and closed at night, much louder than the wake-up and bedtime bells.

A bit off to the side, there are some small one-story houses, some call them villas, others bungalows, where the foreign teachers live. There's also a big house, much larger than the others, that everyone calls the Bungalow. It's reserved for special guests, such as government ministers (should one ever come to stay), or the

Bishop, whose visit is anticipated each year. Occasional tourists from the capital, or from Europe – who've come to see the source of the Nile – are put up there. Between these houses and the lycée, there's a garden with a lawn, flower beds, bamboo groves, and a vegetable patch, of course. The servants who do the gardening grow cabbages, carrots, potatoes, and strawberries; there's even a wheat plot. The tomatoes they harvest here are so pompously plump, they put the *inyanya* – the poor little native tomatoes – to shame. Sister Bursar likes to show visitors around the exotic orchard where the expatriated apricot and peach trees clearly hanker for their native climate. Mother Superior always says that the pupils must get used to civilized food.

A high brick wall was built to discourage intruders and thieves; and at night, guards armed with spears patrol the perimeter and stand watch by the iron gate.

After a while, the people of Nyaminombe stopped noticing the lycée. As far as they're concerned, it's like the huge rocks in Rutare – which seem to have rolled down the mountain and stopped there, in Rutare, for no apparent reason. Yet the construction of the lycée changed many things in the district. A flurry of covered stalls appeared by the builders' campsite, comprising traders who had previously operated close to the mission, and others from goodness knows where. These shops sold the things shops generally sell: individual cigarettes, palm oil, rice, salt, Kraft cheese, margarine, lamp oil, banana beer, Primus lager, Fanta, and sometimes even bread, though not often. There were also bars, referred to as "hotels," serving goat on skewers with grilled bananas and beans, and there were shacks for the loose women who brought the village into disrepute. When the lycée was completed, most of the traders left, except for three bars, two shops, and a tailor: so a new village sprang up by the path leading to the lycée. Even the market, which moved close to the workers' shacks, stayed put, just beyond the stalls.

Yet there was one day that still drew Nyaminombe's idle and curious to the lycée of Our Lady of the Nile, and that was the start of the school year, on a Sunday afternoon in October, at the end of the dry season. They gathered along the side of the track to admire the procession of cars bringing the students to school. There were Mercedes, Range Rovers, and enormous military jeeps, their impatient drivers hooting and waving their arms about, fierce and threatening, as they tried to overtake taxis, pick-ups, and minibuses so overloaded with young women that they struggled to climb the last slope.

One by one, the lycée girls tumbled out before the small throng, which was held back some way from the main gates by two district gendarmes and the mayor himself. A murmur spread through the crowd when Gloriosa stepped out of the black Mercedes with tinted windows, preceded by her mother and followed by Modesta. "She's the spitting image of her father," said the mayor, who had met the great man at a Party rally. "She wears the name her father gave her well: Nyiramasuka, 'She of the Hoe.'" And he repeated this comment loudly enough that the party hacks pressing around him could hear it, sending a swell of admiration through the crowd. Gloriosa certainly did resemble her father, well-built and big-boned: her schoolmates nicknamed her Mastodon under their breath. She wore a navy-blue skirt, just revealing her muscular calves, and a white blouse buttoned to her neck that barely contained her generous bosom. Large round glasses only served to reinforce the unquestionable authority of her gaze. Father Herménégilde abandoned the new girls, the ones entering tenth grade, whom he had been rounding up and reassuring, then motioned to a couple of young lycée hands to take the bags from the chauffeur (who wore a short-sleeved shirt with gold buttons), and rushed toward the new arrivals, striding past Sister Gertrude on reception duty to greet mother and daughter with the customary embraces, entangling himself in the innumerable expressions of welcome that Rwandan courtesy entails. Gloriosa's mother quickly cut him off, explaining that she simply had to greet Mother Superior before dashing back to the capital, where she was expected for dinner at the Belgian Ambassador's, and that she was confident the lycée of Our Lady of the Nile would provide her daughter with the kind of democratic, Christian education appropriate to the female elite of a country that had undergone a social revolution, freeing it from the injustices of a feudal system.

Gloriosa announced that she would stand with Sister Gertrude at the gate, beneath the national flag, to greet the other seniors and let them know that the first meeting of the committee she chaired would take place the following day, in the refectory, after their study hour. Modesta said she'd stand guard duty along with her friend.

Soon after, Goretti also made a grand entrance, perched on the back of a huge military vehicle whose six thick tires took the spectators' breath away. Two soldiers in camouflage fatigues helped her down, hailed the lycée hands to carry her luggage, and bade their passenger farewell with a military salute. Goretti brushed aside Gloriosa's effusive welcome.

"Still prancing about like a minister, I see," Goretti hissed.

"And you, think you're Chief of Staff?" Gloriosa piped back. "Come on, move it, through the gate, and remember, we don't speak anything but French in school: we'll finally get to know what the Ruhengeri girls are saying."

As the Peugeot 404 began the final climb to the lycée, Godelive recognized Immaculée, who was swathed in a wraparound and walking along, with an urchin at her heels carrying her case on his head. She immediately told her driver to stop:

"Immaculée! What happened? Get in, quick! Did your father's car break down? You didn't walk all the way from the capital, did you?"

Immaculée took her wraparound off and got in next to Godelive, while the driver put her case in the trunk. The little porter tapped the glass requesting his tip. Immaculée threw him a coin.

"Don't tell a soul. My boyfriend brought me on his motorbike. He's got a big one, you know. There's no bigger bike than his in all Kigali, perhaps in all Rwanda. He's so proud of it. And I'm so proud to be the girlfriend of the boy with the biggest bike in the country. I get on behind him, and he tears through the streets at full speed, the bike roaring like a lion. Everyone panics and runs for their life, the women all knock over their jugs and baskets. That makes my boyfriend laugh. He promised he'd teach me to ride his bike. Then I'll go even faster than him. Anyway, he told me: 'I'll take you all the way to school on my bike.' Sure, I tell him. I was a bit scared, though, but it was really exciting. Dad was on a business trip to Brussels. I told my mother I was going with a girlfriend. He dropped me off at the last bend, just like I asked. You can imagine the scandal if Mother Superior saw me arrive on a motorbike! I'd be expelled. But look at the state I'm in now, all red with dust. It's horrible! They'll think Dad doesn't have a car anymore, that I hitched a ride on some Toyota pickup, crushed between goats and bananas, and peasant women with their kids on their backs! The shame!"

"You'll take a shower, and I'm sure you've got enough beauty products in that case of yours to put things right."

"That's true. I managed to find some skin-whitening creams, but not that Venus de Milo stuff you get at the market. American ones: tubes of cold cream and green antiseptic soap. My cousin sent me them from the Matonge quarter in Brussels. I'll give you some."

"What would I do with them? There are those who are beautiful, or think they are, and those who are not."

"You look so sad, aren't you glad to be back at school?"

"Why should I be glad to be back at school? I always get the worst grades. The teachers feel sorry for me, but not the rest of you, my dear classmates. It's my dad who wants me to stay on, in spite of everything. Once I get the diploma, he hopes to marry me off to a banker like him. But I'm sure he's got other plans too."

"Cheer up, Godelive. It's our final year and then you'll marry a rich banker."

"Don't make fun of me. Maybe I've got a surprise for you all, a big surprise."

"And what surprise might that be?"

"If I tell you, it won't be a surprise."

Gloriosa welcomed Godelive and Immaculée with disdain, casting a scornful eye over Immaculée's skintight trousers and plunging neckline. Gloriosa wondered why she was covered in dust but decided against asking her right now. She ignored Godelive completely.

"I'm counting on you girls to be real militants," she whispered under her breath. "Not like you were last year. Our Republic requires more than vanity and a banker father."

Immaculée and Godelive pretended not to have heard a word.

With Father Herménégilde as their shepherd, the shy herd of newcomers passed through the gate under Gloriosa's searching gaze:

"Did you notice, Modesta?" She sighed. "The old regime still wields influence in the ministry. They're lax with the quota. If I counted right, and I only counted the girls I know, those I'm sure of, we're way over the percentage that, unfortunately, they've been granted. A fresh invasion! What was the point of our parents' social revolution if we let them carry on like this? I'll be reporting this to my father. But I think we're going to have to take care of things ourselves and get rid of these parasites, once and for all. I told the Bureau of Militant Rwandan Youth about it, and we see eye to eye. They listen to me. It's not for nothing my father named me Nyiramasuka."

Ever since the lycée opened, no one in Nyaminombe had seen a car like the one Frida arrived in. It was very long and low-slung, bright red, with a soft top that had been seen to fold and unfold without anyone touching it. There were only two seats. Both driver and passenger reclined in them as if in bed. It made a noise like thunder, leaping forward in a cloud of red dust. For a moment, it looked as if it would ram the gate and knock Sister Gertrude, Gloriosa, and Modesta flying, but it stopped short, with a hellish screech, right at the foot of the flagpole.

Out stepped a man of a certain age, wearing a three-piece suit (with a floral-patterned waistcoat), large dark glasses with gold-tinted frames, and a crocodile-skin belt with matching shoes. He opened the passenger door and helped Frida extricate herself from the seat in which she was half embedded. Frida smoothed out the creases in her dress, which was as red as the car, and it flared like an umbrella. Beneath her little scarf of purple silk, you could see her brutally straightened hair, stiff, starched, and shimmering in the sun like the asphalt used to resurface some of Kigali's streets not that long ago.

The sports car's driver addressed Sister Gertrude in Swahili (ignoring Gloriosa and Modesta): "I am His Excellency Jean-Baptiste Balimba, the Ambassador of Zaire. I have an appointment with the Mother Superior. Take me to her immediately."

Shocked that anyone would speak to her in that tone, and in Swahili no less, Sister Gertrude hesitated for a moment, but seeing how the man seemed determined to force an entrance, she felt compelled to lead the way.

"Wait for me in the hall," she told Frida. "I'll sort this out, I won't be long."

Gloriosa had pointedly marched out of the gate to greet the nine seniors who were just getting out of a minibus.

"There's our quota," she said, watching as a small truck pulled up, sagging beneath the weight of a wobbly pyramid of barrels and badly stacked cardboard boxes. "See, Modesta, nothing will ever stop the Tutsi from their trafficking: even when they take their daughters back to school, they need to make it worth their while. They unload the goods at the Nyaminombe store, but whose store is it? A Tutsi's, of course; apparently some distant relative of Veronica's father, who himself has a business in Kigali. Oh, she's something, that Veronica; believes she's so beautiful, she'll end up selling herself. And Virginia, her friend, who thinks she's the most intelligent girl in the lycée, simply because all the white teachers dote on her. You know what she's called? Mutamuriza, 'Don't Make Her Cry'! Well, I certainly know how to make her do exactly that. Two Tutsi for twenty pupils is the quota, and because of that I know some real Rwandan girls of the majority people, the people of the hoe, friends of mine, who didn't get a place in high school. As my father likes to tell me, we'll really have to get rid of these quotas one day, it's a Belgian thing!"

Gloriosa's rant was accompanied by little coughs of approval on the part of Modesta, but when she started to lavish overly affectionate hugs of courtesy on the two Tutsi, Modesta moved away.

"The tighter you embrace those snakes," said Gloriosa, once Veronica and Virginia had walked off, "the more you suffocate them, but you, Modesta, you're scared to be mistaken for your half sisters; you sure look like them, and yet I have to put up with you hanging around with me."

"You know I'm your friend."

"Better for you, then, that you always stay my friend," said Gloriosa, hooting with laughter.

At sundown, the clanging bell and the creaking of the closing gates solemnly ushered in the start of the new school year. The monitors had already led the girls to their various dormitories. The seniors were entitled to certain privileges. Their dormitory was divided into alcoves to give each girl some privacy – all relative, since the only thing that separated them from the corridor, where the monitor did her rounds, was a thin green curtain that the sister could pull open at any moment. And although this partitioning of beds, which they called "rooms," was presented by Mother Superior as an example of the progress and emancipation the girls could enjoy thanks to the education provided by the lycée of Our Lady of the Nile, not everyone appreciated it. Late-night gossip and whispers were hushed. Above all, how could a girl sleep on her own? At home, the mothers made sure the younger girls shared a bed or a mat with the older girls. Are sisters really sisters if they don't fall asleep all squashed together? And how can true friendships form without the exchange of confidences on a shared mat? The lycée girls had a hard time falling asleep in their solitary alcoves. They'd listen out for their neighbors' breathing behind the partition, and that reassured them a little. In the tenth-grade dormitory, Sister Gertrude refused to let the boarders move their beds together. "We're at the lycée, here, not at home," she said. "We sleep alone, each in her own bed, like civilized folk."

The girls were asked to put on their uniforms and walk to the chapel two-by-two for Mother Superior and Father Herménégilde's welcome speeches. They sat on the chapel pews, and those girls who didn't yet have uniforms, or had forgotten them, were relegated to the last pews at the back.

Mother Superior and Father Herménégilde appeared suddenly from behind the altar, bowed before the tabernacle and turned to face the pupils. They stood in silence for a while. Father Herménégilde's paternal smile fell on each new face – they'd seated the newcomers in the front row.

Finally, Mother Superior spoke. She welcomed all the pupils, especially those attending the lycée for the first time. She reminded everyone that the lycée of Our Lady of the Nile was founded to train the country's female elite, that those fortunate enough to be there, seated before her, had a duty to become role models for all Rwandan women: not simply to be good wives and mothers, but also good citizens and good Christians – the one not being possible without the other. Women also had a great role to play in the emancipation of the Rwandan people, and it was the girls of the lycée of Our Lady of the Nile who had been chosen to spearhead women's advancement. But she firmly reminded the lycée girls that in the meantime, before they became drivers of change, they must obey the lycée's rules to the letter, with the slightest infringement being severely punished. She also made one thing clear: the only language permitted within the grounds of the lycée was French, except in Kinyarwanda classes of course, but only in class, and nowhere else. Once they married men in positions of high office (and why shouldn't some of the girls end up holding such positions too?), they would be required to use French as their main language. And above all, it was forbidden to utter a single word of Swahili in the lycée, which had been placed under the patronage of the Virgin Mary, for it was a deplorable language, that of the followers of Muhammad. She then wished all the girls a good and studious year, and called on Our Lady of the Nile to bless them.

Father Herménégilde made a long and rambling speech, in which he posited that the people of the hoe who had cleared the huge and hitherto impenetrable forests that covered Rwanda had finally freed themselves from nine hundred years of Hamitic domination. As a humble priest of the indigenous clergy, he himself had contributed, albeit modestly (though he was prepared to share this confidence with them that evening), to the social revolution that had abolished serfdom and drudgery. He may not have been a signatory to the 1957 Bahutu Manifesto, but he had been one of its principal instigators (although he didn't wish to boast): the ideas and demands laid out within it were his. And so he called upon his audience of beautiful young women, so full of promise, who would one day grow into great ladies, to always remember the race they belonged to, the majority race, the sole native one that . . .

Mother Superior, who was rather frightened by this outpouring of eloquence, cut off the orator with a single look.

"And. And now," stammered Father Herménégilde, "I will bless you, and may you receive the protection of Our Lady of the Nile, she who watches over us from so close to our lycée, at the birthplace of that great river."

School Days

The first week of the school year nearly always coincided with the start of the rainy season. If the rains were late, Father Herméné- gilde would ask the pupils to go and offer a bouquet to Our Lady of the Nile, on Sunday after Mass. They'd pick flowers under the anxious, watchful eye of Sister Bursar, who fretted that the girls would destroy her garden, then off they went to lay the wreath at the statue's feet, next to the spring that never ran dry. Most of the time, there was no need for this pilgrimage. A blast of ceaseless thunder rolling and grumbling from the valley meant the rains were on their way. A dark sky, darker than the bottom of an old stockpot, poured down torrents of rain as the children of Nyami- nombe celebrated, dancing and squealing with joy.

For the seniors, lycée life held no further mysteries. They no longer jumped at the noises that woke them each morning: the groan of the gates being opened, the clanging of the school bell, and the whistles the monitors blew as they walked through the dormitories prodding the girls who were slow to rise. Godelive was always the last to get up, whining about wanting to leave the lycée, how she wasn't cut out for studying. Modesta and Immaculée did their best to encourage her, reminding her that Christmas break was approaching, that it was her last year; finally, they would end up yanking her forcibly out of bed. Quickly, they had to take off their nighties, wrap themselves in one of the two large towels that Sister Bursar had given out at the start of the year, tie it under one armpit, then run to the washroom, jostling to reach one of the faucets (showers were taken in the evening). Thanks to her sturdy build, Gloriosa was always the first to lean over the rushing water: everyone else had to make way for her, no matter what. Ablutions over, there was barely enough time to slip into the blue uniform and head to the refectory for tea and porridge. Virginia would swallow it with her eyes shut, forcing herself to think of the delicious *ikivuguto* buttermilk her mother prepared for her each morning during vacation.

She pushed away the little cup filled with powdered sugar, which the other girls fought over so viciously, despite some of them having their own supply, which they poured into their cups to make a sugary gruel. Sugar, a rare commodity in the hills, tasted horribly bitter to Virginia. When she entered sixth grade, she'd never seen as much sugar as she saw here in the cups placed on each of the breakfast tables. She thought of her younger sisters. If only she could bring them the contents of that little cup! Virginia could already imagine the outline of their lips, all white with sugar. She decided to discreetly purloin a few pinches of the precious powder that filled the little cup. It wasn't easy, because this coveted treat was very closely watched. What's more, being Tutsi, Virginia received the cup last, and there were only a few grains of sugar remaining at the bottom. She carefully scooped them up with her teaspoon, and instead of pouring the sugar into her bowl, slipped it furtively into one of the pockets of her uniform as quickly as possible. She emptied her pocket every night, and by the end of term she'd managed to fill half an envelope. But Dorothée, who sat next to her, saw what she was up to, and just before breaking for vacation, she said:

"You're a thief. I'm going to tell on you."

"Me, a thief?"

"Yes, you steal sugar every morning. You think I don't notice. You want to sell it back home in the countryside, at the market, during vacation."

"It's for my little sisters. There's no sugar in the countryside. Don't tell on me."

"Perhaps we can make a deal. You're top of the class in French. If you write my next essay, I won't say a thing."

"Let me take the sugar for my little sisters."

"If you write my essays for the rest of the year."

"I'll do it, I swear, for the rest of the year."

The teacher was amazed at Dorothée's sudden progress. He suspected some kind of cheating was going on but didn't care to find out more. From then on, Dorothée's grades in French were the best in the class.

The bell clanged again. Lessons were about to start: French, Math, Religion, Health and Hygiene, History, Geography, Physics, Physical Education, English, Kinyarwanda, Sewing, French, Cooking, History, Geography, Physics, Health and Hygiene, Math, Religion, Cooking, English, Sewing, French, Religion, Physical Education, French . . .

The days wore on.

There were only two Rwandans on the entire teaching staff of the lycée of Our Lady of the Nile: Sister Lydwine, and the Kinyarwanda teacher, naturally. Sister Lydwine taught History and Geography, but she made a clear distinction between the two subjects: History meant Europe, and Geography, Africa. Sister Lydwine was passionate about the Middle Ages. Her classes were all about castles, keeps, arrow slits, machicolations, drawbridges, and bartizans. Knights set off on crusades, with the Pope's blessing, to liberate Jerusalem and massacre the Saracens, while others fought duels with lances for the eyes of ladies wearing pointy hats. Sister Lydwine talked of Robin Hood, Ivanhoe, and Richard the Lionheart. "I've seen them in movies!" said Veronica, unable to contain herself.

"Will you please be quiet!" said Sister Lydwine crossly. "They lived a very long time ago, before your ancestors had even set foot in Rwanda."

Africa had no history, because Africans could neither read nor write before the missionaries opened their schools. Besides, it was the Europeans who had discovered Africa and dragged it into history. And if there had been any kings in Rwanda, it was better to forget them, for the country was now a Republic. Africa had mountains, volcanoes, rivers, lakes, deserts, forests, and even a few cities. It was just a question of memorizing their names and finding them on the map: Kilimanjaro, Tamanrasset, Karisimbi, Timbuktu, Tanganyika, Muhabura, Fouta Djallon, Kivu, Ouagadougou. But there was a kind of large lizard in the middle. Sister Lydwine lowered her voice and, casting suspicious glances at the hallway, explained that Africa was breaking in two, and that one day Rwanda would find itself by the sea, though on which side of the continent, left or right, she really couldn't say. To her chagrin, the whole class erupted into laughter. Clearly the whites never stopped coming up with far-fetched tales to scare the poor Africans.

Monsieur Van der Putten was the math teacher. His pupils had never heard him utter a single word of French. He communicated with his class only through numbers (French numbers, he couldn't get around that) and above all by covering the blackboard with algebraic formulas or drawing geometrical shapes in every color of chalk. However, he did hold long conversations with Brother Auxile in a dialect that must have belonged to one of the Belgian tribes. But when he addressed Mother Superior, it was apparently in a slightly different dialect. Visibly annoyed, Mother Superior answered him in French, articulating every syllable. Monsieur Van der Putten walked off mumbling (in his incomprehensible dialect) words that were perhaps not quite as rude as they seemed to the listener.

Religious Studies was obviously Father Herménégilde's domain. Using proverbs, he demonstrated how Rwandans had always worshipped a single God, a God named Imana who was like a twin brother to Yahweh, the Hebrews' God in the Bible. The ancient Rwandans were already Christians without realizing it, and so they waited impatiently for the missionaries to arrive and baptize them, except that the devil got there first and corrupted their innocence. Wearing the mask of Ryangombe, he induced them into nocturnal orgies where countless demons took possession of their bodies and their souls, forcing them into obscene utterances and the committing of acts that decency forbade him from specifying in the presence of such chaste young ladies. Father Herménégilde crossed himself several times as he pronounced the cursed name of Ryangombe.

Happy the teacher fortunate enough to teach in Rwanda! There are no calmer, more obedient, more attentive pupils than Rwandan pupils. The lycée of Our Lady of the Nile illustrated these wise words perfectly, except for one class, that of Miss South, the English teacher, where there reigned, not quite chaos, but a certain agitation. It's true that the lycée girls didn't really understand why they were obliged to learn a language no one spoke anywhere in Rwanda, although you might overhear a little in Kigali, spoken by a few Pakistani immigrants recently arrived from Uganda, or (and this was a good indication of what kind of language it was) by Protestant pastors who, as Father Herménégilde liked to point out, forbade worship of the Virgin Mary. There was little about Miss South's physique or behavior to make the language of Shakespeare appealing. She was a tall woman, dry and abrasive, with short hair except for one long strand – which she was forever trying to tame – that flapped against her oval glasses. She always wore a blue pleated skirt, faded from repeated washing, and a blouse with a pale-lilac floral print that was buttoned all the way to the neck. She'd clatter into class, fling her beat-up leather bag on the table, pull out a sheaf of papers, then stumble around the classroom, bumping into desks, as she handed them out. The pupils stared at her intently, cheeks resting on their right palms, waiting for the fall that never came. During the lesson, she would recite rather than read the stenciled text, before getting the class to repeat in unison what she had just said. The pupils wondered aloud whether she was blind, crazy, or drunk. Frida said she was drunk, confidently claiming that the English drink very strong spirits from dawn till dusk, spirits that were much stronger than *urwarwa*, like Johnnie Walker, which her ambassador friend had given her to taste, and which made her giddy. Sometimes Miss South tried to get the class to sing:

> *My bonnie lies over the ocean*
> *My bonnie lies over the sea . . .*

But this raised such a cacophony that the teacher from the class next door rushed in to restore a little quiet. "At last!" sighed the pupils.

It was the third year that French teachers had been working at Our Lady of the Nile. When Mother Superior received the Minister's letter announcing that three Frenchmen would be arriving at the school as volunteer teachers, the news filled her with worry. She confided her misgivings and fears about these young men to Father Herménégilde: they were clearly inexperienced, since the letter specified they were coming in their capacity as "volunteers on active national service," one of those odd expressions the French are so fond of inventing.

"So," concluded Mother Superior, "these are young men who didn't want to do their military service; they're antimilitarists, possibly conscientious objectors, or Jehovah's Witnesses – that's all we need! It doesn't bode well. And you know what happened in France, Father Herménégilde, not so long ago: students in the streets, strikes, demonstrations, riots, barricades, revolution! We'll have to keep an eye on these gentlemen, monitor what they say in class, so they don't spread subversion and atheism in our pupils' minds."

"There isn't much we can do about it," replied Father Herménégilde. "If they're sending us these Frenchmen, it's a matter of politics and diplomacy. Surely our small country needs to build broader relationships. After all, there's more than just Belgium . . ."

The first two Frenchmen were delivered to the lycée by a car from their embassy, which reassured Mother Superior to a certain extent. Naturally, they wore no ties, and one of them, rather worryingly, had a guitar among his belongings, but they seemed reasonably polite, shy, and slightly dazed to find themselves suddenly transplanted to these remote mountains in a country they'd never heard of in farthest Africa. "Monsieur Lapointe insisted on coming here under his own steam," explained the Cultural Attaché a little vaguely. "He should arrive before nightfall or tomorrow at the very latest."

The third Frenchman did indeed arrive the next morning, in the back of a Toyota. He kindly helped the women with babies on their backs to climb out. The lycée guards pulled the ever-vocal gates wide open for him, as if greeting an official vehicle. It was the second lesson of the day, and the girls, or at least those sitting closest to the windows, saw a very tall, very skinny young man striding across the courtyard, dressed in jeans that had lost all their color, and a short-sleeved khaki shirt that hung open across his hairy chest. His only luggage was a backpack decorated with numerous patches. But what really startled those girls who were lucky enough to see him, making them squeal with surprise, causing all the others to jump up and rush to the windows, in spite of their teachers' protests, was his hair, his thick, blond, wavy hair, which hung halfway down his back.

"Well, it must be a girl," Godelive said.

"Not at all, you saw very well from the front, it's a man," argued Frida.

"He's a hippie," Immaculée explained. "The young people in America are all like that now."

Sister Gertrude ran to warn Mother Superior:

"*Mon Dieu*! The Frenchman, Mother, he's here!"

"Well, what about the Frenchman? Show him in."

"Oh, *mon Dieu*, Reverend Mother! The Frenchman, wait till you see him!"

Mother Superior had the greatest difficulty suppressing a gasp of horror when the new teacher entered her study.

"I'm Olivier Lapointe," said the Frenchman nonchalantly. "I've been posted here. This is the lycée of Our Lady of the Nile, right?"

Stunned with indignation, Mother Superior was lost for words, and in order to gather her senses, she turned to Sister Gertrude:

"Sister Gertrude, please show Monsieur to his lodgings."

Kanyarushatsi (Mr. Hair), as the girls called him, remained closeted in his bungalow for two weeks. They told him they were putting the finishing touches to the timetable. Nearly every day, a delegation sent by Mother Superior – Father Herménégilde, Sister Gertrude, Sister Lydwine, the Belgian teachers, the two other Frenchmen, and, finally, Mother Superior herself – attempted, on the pretext of a courtesy visit, to persuade him to get a haircut. Mr. Hair was prepared to cede on every other issue: wear a shirt and tie, and decent trousers. But when it came to his long hair, he was quite intransigent. They suggested he cut it to at least shoulder length. He refused point-blank. Never would he let a single hair be touched. His long locks were his one pride, the masterpiece of his youth, his whole reason for living, and he wouldn't give it up for anything in the world.

Mother Superior bombarded the ministry with desperate letters. The French teacher's shamefully long hair was a threat to every moral, both civic and Christian, and imperiled the future of

Rwanda's female elite. The Minister wrote an embarrassed letter to the French ambassador and his cultural Attaché, who returned to the lycée and threatened Mr. Hair. In vain. Despite the close surveillance placed on his bungalow, the lycée girls came and hovered around it. Whenever there was a sunny spell, he was often seen drying his long, golden curls outside after a shampoo. Some girls even dared to gesture and call to him from afar: "Kanya-rushatsi! Kanyarushatsi!" The lycée staff eventually lost heart and allowed him into the classroom. They needed a math teacher. Yet the pupils were very disappointed with his performance. In class, he never budged from his equations. He was actually quite similar to Monsieur Van der Putten, except that when he turned around to write on the blackboard, the girls gazed, enraptured, at his long flowing mane. When Kanyarushatsi left the room at the end of class, the most shameless of the seniors swarmed about him and, under the pretext of asking him questions about elements they hadn't understood, tried to touch his hair. He answered as quickly as he could, without daring to look at the cluster of insistent young women jostling him. He finally managed to extricate himself from this pack of purportedly curious girls, striding off down the hallway to escape them.

At the end of the year he was sent back to France. "We were mere tenth graders then," said a regretful Immaculée, "but if he were still around, I'd know just how to tame him now."

"They haven't touched a thing, again," bemoaned Sister Bénigne, assigned to the kitchen to help old Sister Kizito, whose hands trembled and who needed two canes to walk. "The dishes come back half eaten. Are they scared I'll poison them? Do they take me for a poisoner? I'd really like to know who put that into their heads! Is it because I'm from Gisaka?"

"Don't you worry now," said Sister Kizito in a reassuring voice. "You'll see, Gisaka or no Gisaka, this time next week their suitcases will be empty, and whether they like your cooking or not, they'll be forced to eat it. They'll lick the plates clean."

Before returning their daughters to school, the girls' mothers had indeed filled their suitcases with the most delectable food a Rwandan mother could imagine and prepare.

"They make them eat nothing but white people's food at the lycée," they'd say. "Unfit for Rwandans, especially young women – some say it could make them infertile."

So suitcases became well-stocked pantries filled by doting mothers: beans and cassava paste, with a special sauce, in little enameled containers decorated with large flowers and wrapped in a piece of cloth; bananas slowly baked overnight; *ibisheke*, sugarcane you chew and chew until the pure fibrous marrow fills your mouth with its sweet juice; red *gahungezi* sweet potatoes; corncobs; peanuts; and even, for the city girls, doughnuts of every color under the sun – a secret Swahili recipe – avocados you can only buy at Kigali markets, and extra-salty, red-roasted peanuts.

At night, as soon as the monitor had left the dorm, the feast began. The suitcases were opened, and all the victuals laid out on the beds. One of the girls would check that the monitor was fast asleep, but some of the monitors, like Sister Rita, weren't fools and were quite willing to be corrupted in order to join the banquet. An assessment was made of everyone's provisions, and it was decided what should be eaten first, before the evening's menu was planned. Any selfish, greedy girl who tried to keep a little of her pantry for herself, and deprive the communal banquet, was roundly condemned.

Alas! The supplies soon ran out, and after two or three weeks there was nothing left but a few handfuls of peanuts reserved for emergency consolation on really bad days. The girls would have to resign themselves to eating whatever was served in the refectory: tasteless bulgur; a yellow paste, with the sonorous name "polenta," that stuck to the palate and that Father Angelo – a regular guest from the neighboring mission – wolfed down with relish; soft little oily fish out of cans; and sometimes, on Sundays and holidays, meat from who knows what sort of animal called corned beef . . .

"Everything the whites eat," moaned Godelive, "comes out of cans, even the sliced mango and pineapple swimming in syrup, and the only real bananas they serve us are the sweet bananas at the end of the meal, but that's not how you eat bananas. As soon as I get home for vacation, me and my mother will prepare real bananas. We'll oversee the kitchen hand as he peels and cooks them, in water with tomatoes. Then my mother and I will add everything else: onions, palm oil, very mild *irengarenga* spinach, quite bitter *isogi* leaves, and small dried *ndagala* fish. It'll be a real feast, with my mother and sisters."

"You don't know anything," Gloriosa said. "What you need is peanut sauce, *ikinyiga*, and then cook slowly, really slowly, so that the sauce infuses right to the heart of the bananas."

"But if you cook with Butane gas and a saucepan like they do in the city," Modesta butted in, "the bananas will cook too fast, and they won't be soft and creamy. You need to use a clay pot and charcoal. It takes a very long time. I'll give you the real recipe, it's my mother's. First of all, you mustn't peel the bananas. You put a little water in a big pot, then lay the bananas on top, nice and tight, and cover them with a thick layer of banana leaves; it must be airtight, so use leaves that aren't torn. Then weigh them down with a shard of pottery. Now wait, a long time. It's got to cook nice and slow, but if you're patient you'll get lovely white bananas, soft and creamy all the way through. And you have to eat them with some *ikivuguto* buttermilk, and invite your neighbors."

"My poor Modesta," said Goretti, "your mother is always so fussy, with her lovely white immaculate bananas, served with milk! You always take after your mother. I'll tell you what to make for your father: dark red bananas that have soaked up the bean juice. I'm sure your mother wouldn't touch them, but when the houseboy prepares some for your father, you'll be obliged to try them. Teach your mother the recipe: she must peel them, and then, when the beans are almost done but the pot's still half full of water, throw them in the pot so they absorb all the remaining liquid. The bananas will turn red, brown even, that's what makes them thick and succulent! Bananas for true Rwandans who've got the strength to wield a hoe!"

"You're all city girls," said Virginia, "or from rich families. You've never eaten bananas in the fields. That's where they're at their best! Often when we're working in the fields and we don't have time to go home, we'll light a little fire and grill a couple of bananas, not in the flames of course, but in the red-hot embers. Yet there's something even better: when I was a little girl, my mother would sometimes give me and my girlfriends a few bananas. We'd head into the fields after the sorghum harvest and dig a small hole, then light a fire in the hole with dried banana leaves. After it died down, we'd remove the embers, but the hole would still be glowing red. So we'd line it with a fresh green banana leaf, place the bananas in the hole and cover them with the hot earth. Then you just put a banana leaf on top and sprinkle it with a little water. When the leaf is fairly dry, you open up the hole. The banana skins look like a soldier's camouflage gear, and the inside is so tender, it just melts in your mouth! I don't think I've ever eaten bananas so tasty."

"So what did you come to the lycée for?" asked Gloriosa. "You should have stayed in the sticks munching bananas in the fields. You would have made room for a real Rwandan from the majority people."

"Sure, I'm from the country and I'm not ashamed of it, but I am ashamed of what I just said and of what we've all been saying. Do Rwandans ever talk about what they eat? It's shameful to talk about that. It's shameful even to eat in front of others, to open your mouth in front of someone, yet that's what we all do here every day!"

"It's true," said Immaculée. "Whites have no modesty. I hear them when my father invites them over to talk business. He's got no choice. The whites never stop talking about what they eat, what they have eaten, and what they will eat."

"And the Zairians," Goretti said, looking at Frida, "they eat termites, crickets, snakes, and monkeys, and they're proud of it!"

"They'll be ringing soon for the refectory," said Gloriosa. "Come along. And you, Virginia, you'll have no choice but to open your mouth in front of us and eat up the leftovers of real Rwandan girls."

Rain

The rain fell on the lycée of Our Lady of the Nile. How many days and weeks had it been? Everyone had stopped counting. Mountains and clouds were but a single grumbling chaos, as if on the first or last day of the world. The rain streamed down the face of Our Lady of the Nile, washing off her black mask. The supposed source of the Nile flooded over the edge of the basin in a raging torrent. Passersby on the path – in Rwanda there are always passersby on the path, though you never know where they're coming from or where they're going – took shelter beneath giant banana leaves that the thin film of water changed into green mirrors.

For many long months, rain becomes the Sovereign of Rwanda, a far greater ruler than the former King or the current President. Her coming is eagerly awaited and entreated. Famine or plenty, it's Rain who will decide. Rain, the good omen of a fertile marriage. First rains, at the end of the dry season, making children dance as they turn their faces skyward to receive the fat drops for which they've longed. Shameless rain, revealing the budding curves of all young women beneath their drenched wraparounds. Violent, capricious, punctilious Mistress, pitter-pattering on every sheet-metal roof, on those sheltering in the banana groves or in the muddy neighborhoods of the capital. She who casts her net over the lake, and diminishes the volcanoes' hugeness; she who reigns over the vast forests of the Congo, the very guts of Africa. Rain, endless Rain, unto the ocean that bore her.

"Maybe it rains like this the world over," said Modesta, "maybe it will just keep on raining and never stop, maybe it's Noah's flood all over again."

"Just imagine, girls," said Gloriosa, "if it was the flood, we'd soon be the only ones left on Earth, the lycée's way too high up to drown, it'd be like the Ark. We'd be alone on Earth."

"And when the water ebbs away – because it's bound to one day – it'd be up to us to repopulate the earth. But how will we manage if there are no boys left?" Frida said. "The white teachers would have left ages ago to drown back home, and I for one won't have Brother Auxile or Father Herménégilde."

"C'mon," said Virginia. "The flood's an *abapadri* tale. Where I come from, up on my hill, we abandon the fields as soon as it rains and gather around the fire. Vacation time. No need to fetch water, because we make banana-leaf gutters to catch the rain. We can shower and do our washing at home. We spend our time roasting corn as we roast our feet. But be careful, if the cob bursts and the kernels fly, that attracts lightning. And my mother says: 'Don't laugh, those who show their teeth, especially those with red gums, they'll bring on lightning.'"

"And we have the *abavubyi* in Rwanda, the rainmakers," said Veronica. "They're the ones who control the rain, making her start or stop. But perhaps they've forgotten how to make her stop. Or else they're taking revenge on the missionaries who make fun of them and denounce them to the district authorities."

"And do you believe in those *abavubyi*?"

"I'm not sure, but I know one, an old woman. I went to see her with Immaculée, she lives nearby."

"Tell us."

"One Sunday after Mass, Immaculée told me: 'I want to go see Kagabo, the healer. You know, the one who sells strange medicines at the market. I'm a little scared to go see him alone. Want to come along?' Of course I was ready to accompany Immaculée; I was curious to see what she was up to with that witch doctor the Sisters call the devil's henchman. You know Kagabo, you see him at the market, right at the end of the row of women selling peas and firewood. A little apart, but no one bothers him; the district police officers don't go anywhere near him, and his customers prefer no one notice them. He lays out his wares in front of him on a piece of matting; they're pretty scary looking. I know that some people will ask me what the point is of those oddly shaped roots and all those herbs and dried leaves and the little shells that come from far away, from the sea, as well as glass beads like the necklaces our grandmothers used to wear, the skins of serval cats, snake skins and lizard skins, small hoes, arrowheads, little bells, copper-wire bracelets, powder in banana-bark packets, and who knows what else. I don't think he has many clients. The ones who are seeking out Kagabo only pretend they've come to buy something; for more complicated matters, they make appointments to see him at his home, wherever that is, to heal themselves with his little jars of Nile water, to cast a spell, or be freed from one, and for even more serious things.

"We walked up to Kagabo, trembling a little. Immaculée was too afraid to address him. He eventually spotted us and beckoned. 'What can I do for you, my belles demoiselles?' Quickly, Immaculée whispered: 'I need your help, Kagabo. You see, the thing is, I've got a suitor, in the capital. I'm scared he'll chase after other girls, that he'll dump me. Give me something to keep my sweetheart, so he has eyes only for me, so he doesn't see any other girls, so there's only one girl for him in all the world. I don't want to see another girl on his motorbike.' Kagabo answered: 'I deal with sickness, I'm a healer, love problems don't concern me. But I know someone who can help you out, and that's Nyamirongi, the rainmaker. She's doesn't just deal with clouds. Give me a hundred francs and I'll take you to see her next Sunday; you can bring your friend along, but she'll have to pay a hundred francs too. Come when the market packs up and we'll go to Nyamirongi's.'

"So the following Sunday, me and Immaculée went to the far side of the market. Kagabo had already tucked away his witch's wares in an old bag woven from fig-tree bark. 'Hey, you two, follow me, and hurry it up. Do you have my money, and more for Nyamirongi?' We handed him our hundred-franc bills and off we went, along the track that led down to the village. We soon left it and proceeded along the ridgeline. Kagabo walked very fast; it was as if his huge bare feet hardly touched the grass. 'Hurry up, hurry up,' he repeated, over and over again. We struggled to keep up, out of breath. Then we reached a kind of plateau. From there we saw the lake, the distant volcanoes, and on the other shore, the mountains of the Congo. But we didn't stop to admire the view. Kagabo pointed out a little hut to us, behind a rocky mound, like those of the Batwa people; a white smoke drifted out of it, spreading and mixing with the clouds. 'Wait,' said Kagabo. 'I'll see if she'll let you in.' We waited a long time. We could hear whispers, moans, and high-pitched laughter from inside the hut. Kagabo emerged: 'Come,' he said. 'She's finally put her pipe down. She'll happily see you.'

"We ducked to enter the hut. It was very dark and filled with smoke. Eventually we spotted glowing red coals, and behind them, a shape wrapped in a blanket. A voice from under the covers spoke: 'Come closer, come closer.' Kagabo motioned for us to sit down; then the covers parted slightly and we saw an old woman's face, wrinkled, crumpled like a shriveled passion fruit, but with eyes that burned as bright as embers. Nyamirongi, for it was she, asked our names. How she laughed when Immaculée told her she was called Mukagatare, 'You may not yet be "She of Purity," but that will come one day.' She asked the names of our parents and grandparents, then pondered for a moment, holding her little head in hands that seemed so big. Then she recited the names of our ancestors, even those our parents couldn't have known. 'You're not from very good families,' she concluded, chuckling. 'But nowadays they say it no longer matters.'

"She turned to Immaculée: 'So, Kagabo tells me it's you who wants to see me.'

"Immaculée explained to her that she had a sweetheart in the capital, but that she'd heard, or rather some friends had written to tell her, that they'd seen him with other girls on his motorbike. She wanted Nyamirongi to put a stop to that, to make her sweetheart quit going out with them, so he would be hers, and hers alone.

"'Right,' said Nyamirongi. 'That can be arranged. But tell me, have you slept with your sweetheart?'

"'No! Never!'

"'He's fondled your breasts, at least?'

"'Well, a bit, yes,' Immaculée replied, bowing her head.

"'And elsewhere, too?'

"'A bit, a bit,' Immaculée murmured.

"'Right, I see . . . That can be arranged.'

"Nyamirongi rummaged in the various calabashes and pots that were piled up all around her. She took out some seeds, which she examined for a long while, then selected a few and placed them in a little mortar. She crushed the seeds to a powder, and spat on them, all the while mumbling some inaudible words, and made a thick concoction that she wrapped in a piece of banana leaf, like cassava paste.

"'Here, take this. You're going to write to your sweetheart – you're a lycée girl, you can write, even women know how to write these days! The paste will be dry in three days, you'll grind it to a powder and slip some into an envelope, but don't forget, before you do that, rub some over your breasts, and the rest. When your suitor opens the letter, he'll breathe in the powder, and I promise, you'll keep your sweetheart all to yourself, he'll stop going off with other girls. Now give me five hundred francs, and he'll have eyes for you alone, he'll think only of you, you'll hold him captive; I give you the word of Nyamirongi, daughter of Kitatire, but you must let him caress you all over, and I mean all over, understand?'

"She picked up her pipe and drew three puffs on it. Immaculée handed her a five-hundred-franc note, which she tucked beneath her blanket. Then she turned to face me:

"'And why did you come? What do you want from me?'

"'They said you control the rain. I want to see how you do it.'

"'You're too curious. I don't control the rain: I talk to her, and she answers. I always know where she is, and if I ask her to come or go, and if she feels like it, she does what I ask. You young girls at the *abapadri* school, you no longer know anything. Back when I was young, before the Belgians and the chief of the *abapadri* ousted King Yuhi Musinga, they respected me, even then. They knew of my power because it came from my mother, who received it from her own mother, who had received it from her mother, who herself received it from our ancestor Nyiramvura, "She of the Rain." I lived in a large enclosure at the foot of the mountain, a large enclosure near a watering hole. When the rains were late, and you know what the rain is like, she never knows when she's due, the chiefs led their cattle to my watering hole, which never ran dry. They brought their young dancers, the *intore*. And they'd say: "Nyamirongi, tell us where the rain is, tell her to come and we'll give you cows, jugs of mead, and cloth so you can dress as if you were at court with the King." And I replied: "First, you must dance for the rain, after your cattle have slaked their thirst; your *intore* must dance for the rain." And the *intore* danced before me, and when they had danced enough, I told the chiefs: "Return to your enclosures, for the rain is coming, she'll catch up with you before you get there." And the rain fell on the cattle, on the beans, on the corn, on the taro; it fell on the sons of Gihanga: on the Tutsi, on the Hutu, on the Batwa. I saved the country often, which is why they called me Umubyeyi, Mother, mother of the country. But when the Bazungu gave the Drum to the new King, they chased me from my enclosure, they wanted to hang me, and I hid in the forest for a long time. Now that I am old, I live alone in this Batwa hut. People go to the *abapadri* to make them bring the rain. But do these whites know how to talk to the rain? The rain hasn't been to school; she won't listen to them: the rain does as she pleases. You need to know how to talk to her. So some people still seek me out, like your friend here. And not just about the rain. If you want to know how I talk to the rain and how the rain, if she is so inclined, obeys me, then dance for the rain, dance here before me for the rain. It's been so long since anyone danced before me for the rain.'

"'Nyamirongi! You can see very well I can't dance in this lycée uniform, and your hut is much too small, but please, tell me anyway where the rain is now.'

"'Well, if you don't wish to dance, give me five hundred francs and I'll tell you where the rain is.'

"I gave her the five hundred francs.

"'Right, you're a good girl. I'll show you what I'm capable of.'

She stretched out her right arm and made a fist, but with her forefinger pointing toward the hut's rounded roof. A long nail stuck out like an eagle's talon. She moved her arm so that the forefinger with its long nail covered the four points of the compass. Then she drew her arm back beneath the blanket.

"I know where the rain is. She is over the lake, and she tells me she's coming. Leave now, quickly, run fast before she catches you.

I see her, she's coming, she's crossing the lake. Give me another five hundred francs if you don't want to be struck by lightning. You made the rain angry because you didn't dance for her. Give me five hundred francs and the lightning will spare you.'

"'Hurry,' said Kagabo. 'Do as she says and let's go.'

"We ran and ran down the mountain and down the track. Clouds were massing, rising toward us. Thunder rumbled. Just as we entered the lycée gates, a torrential rain began to fall, and lightning ripped across the sky."

The girls remained silent for a long while, listening to the obstinate beating of the rain.

"I think that Nyamirongi and the rain have much to talk about," said Modesta finally. "This rain will never end."

"She'll end like she does every year, with the dry season," said Gloriosa, "but tell me, Veronica, did Immaculée get her sweetheart back?"

"He came up to see her immediately. The folks in Nyaminombe saw a bike streak past, a huge one like they'd never seen before. It caused everyone to flee, and a little girl broke her pitcher, but of course her sweetheart didn't turn up at the lycée. They'd arranged to meet in that abandoned shepherd's shack, near the spring – you know what people do there. Immaculée followed Nyamirongi's advice, perhaps a bit too closely, I fear."

"You're too curious, Veronica," said Gloriosa. "It will get you into trouble, visiting witches like that. I bet you danced before that witch. Only a Tutsi would dance for the devil. I could tell on you, but I don't want to cause any trouble for Immaculée. Her father's a businessman. My dad says he's generous to the Party, after all. But if that old woman can bring lovers back together, if she can control the rain, then I'll go see Nyamirongi too: maybe she can take care of a few things in politics."

Isis

"Listen, Virginia, there's something I want to tell you. But don't breathe a word to anyone."

"You know we Tutsi never reveal our secrets, Veronica. We're taught to keep our mouths shut. We have to, if we want to stay alive. You know what our parents tell us: 'Your tongue is your enemy.' If you think you've got a secret to share, you can trust me, I can keep a secret."

"Well, listen carefully. You know how on Sundays I like to go for a wander up the mountain by myself. You all resent me for it, but I never feel like going to the boutique with the other girls, or to the tailor's, to find out who's ordered a new dress. I'd rather be alone, so I no longer have to see all those girls who hate us. When I get up into the mountains, I sit on a rock and close my eyes. There's no one around, just the twinkling of beautiful stars beneath my eyelids. And sometimes I imagine myself in a happier life, the kind you only get in movies, I guess . . ."

"Is that all you have to tell me?"

"No, hang on. I'd gone a long way, toward the massive Rutare rocks, so far that I no longer knew where I was. Nobody lives up there. Suddenly, I hear the noise of an engine behind me, clanking like an old jalopy. Out here, in the middle of nowhere, there's only one vehicle that makes that sound: Monsieur de Fontenaille's jeep. And sure enough, the jeep overtakes me and screeches to a stop just in front of me. Monsieur de Fontenaille doffs his hat.

"'Greetings, Mademoiselle, you're so far from the lycée, are you lost? Jump in, we'll take a little tour in my jeep and I'll drive you back to the track.'

"I'm scared, my heart's thumping like it wants to leap out of my chest, so I make a run for it, with the jeep racing after me.

"'Hey, don't be scared, I wish you no harm. And, anyway, I recognize you, I know who you are. You stood out from the other girls at the pilgrimage. I've done portraits of you. Come, I really must show them to you.'

"I'm so out of breath I can't run any more, and the jeep stops beside me.

"'Yes', says Monsieur de Fontenaille. 'Yes, it's definitely you, the one I spotted, the one I've been looking for, the one I need. And it is She who has sent you.'

"He looks at me intently, as if fascinated by my face. I lower my eyes of course, but I sense that my curiosity will get the better of my fear.

"'What do you want with me?'

"'Nothing bad, quite the opposite. My intentions are all good, I swear. I won't touch you, I promise. Trust me. Hop in, I'll take you to see my house. Once we get there, you'll see yourself as you were meant to be. The temple has awaited its goddess for such a long time.'

"'Awaited its goddess?'

"'You'll see for yourself.'

"My curiosity won over, just as I'd feared.

"'Okay, but you have to take me back to the lycée by six. And no one must see us.'

"'I'll take you back, discreetly.'

"Slope after slope, the jeep climbed then hurtled down, I don't know how many times, as it jolted, squealed, and spluttered. A hell of a noise. Fontenaille laughed, watching me all the while. It seemed like the vehicle was driving itself. At last, we reached a dirt path and passed beneath an arch, a bit like on Rwanda Day, but this one was made of iron. I had time to read the sign that said FONTENAILLE ESTATE, and above the inscription, I thought I glimpsed another smaller sign with some sort of Holy Virgin wearing a hat with cattle horns painted on it, like the one Fontenaille showed me later inside his villa. We drove between rows of ill-maintained coffee bushes, then past a series of identical small brick dwellings that appeared to be abandoned. We stopped in front of the large house.

"'Come on,' Fontenaille says, 'I'll give you a tour of the estate and show you what could be yours.'

"I was still a little scared, and I still didn't understand what he was saying, or what he wanted, but it was too late to back out and I was really eager to know what it all meant. Whatever happens, I thought, I could always find a way to get out of there . . .

"We crossed the *barza* and entered the large living room, where a servant rushed up to us with glasses of orange juice. He wore a white uniform with gold epaulettes. Fontenaille didn't take his eyes off me as I drank my glass of orangeade. Myself, I looked at the antelope horns, the elephant tusks, and the zebra pelt hanging on the wall.

"'Please, ignore all that bric-a-brac, the animal hides, I put them up for people who no longer visit me. These are all beasts I wish I hadn't killed. Now follow me.'

"We took a long corridor that led to a garden. Behind the bamboo groves, there was a small lake overgrown with papyrus sedge and, farther back, a sort of chapel, but not like one of those missionary churches. It was a rectangular building with columns all around. As I got closer, I saw that the columns were sculpted: they looked like papyrus sedge. Inside, the walls were covered with paintings: on one side there were cows with huge *inyambo* horns, and warriors like our *intore* dancers, with an imposing figure in the foreground that must've been the King, with a crown of pearls like Mwami Musinga wore. On the other side was a procession of women, young black women who resembled the queens of old. It looked like they were walking behind each other, their faces in profile. They all wore the same tight dresses, bare-breasted; the dresses were transparent, and in the folds you could see the curves of their stomachs, and their legs. On their heads they had these wigs that didn't look like hair, more like birds. On the back wall was a kind of large Holy Virgin, black as Our Lady of the Nile, dressed like the women on the wall, but painted full face and wearing a hat similar to the one I'd seen at the entrance to the estate: two cow horns and a disc shining bright as sunlight. I felt as if the Lady were looking at me with her big black eyes, like a living person. In front of her, on a dais, was an armchair with a very high back, and gilded like the one the Bishop sits on in the cathedral. On the seat lay the strange hat.

"'Look closely,' said Monsieur de Fontenaille. 'Do you recognize her? Do you recognize yourself?'

"I didn't know how to reply.

"'Look closely,' he said again. 'It's the Lady of the Nile, the real one. Don't you think you look like her?'

"'So what? She's black like me. But apart from that? I'm Veronica, I'm not the Virgin Mary.'

"'No, you're not the Virgin Mary, and neither is She. And if you are worthy, I would like to reveal her true name to you, which is also your own.'

"'My real name, the one my father gave me, is Tumurinde. You know what it means: "Protect Her."'

"'You can count on me to fulfill your father's wishes: you're so precious to me. But there's another name I know that is earmarked for you, that awaits you. I'll explain everything if you come back and see me.'

"I still understood nothing of what he was saying, but I was increasingly curious to know what it all meant, and I answered him before I had time to think:

"'I'll return next Sunday, but with a friend. I'm not coming back on my own.'

"'If your friend looks like you, then you can bring her, but only if she looks like you. There's a place for her, too.'

"'I'll bring her. But it's late – you need to take me back to the lycée, and without anyone seeing us!'

"'My old jeep's not too fond of dirt roads.'

"He dropped me off behind the guest bungalow, just before six, and sped away."

"What a strange story," said Virginia. "That white guy is really crazy. Who are you going to take with you?"

"You, of course. You'll come to the white guy's place with me next Sunday. We'll play goddess. You'll see, it's like being in a movie."

"Don't you think it's risky? You know what whites do with girls they lure back to their places. Whites think they can get away with anything out here, that they can do everything that's forbidden back home."

"Not at all, you've nothing to fear. Fontenaille is just a crazy old guy. But he kept his word, didn't lay a finger on me. I'm telling you, he thinks I'm a goddess. It'll be the same with you. You know what whites say about the Tutsi. I looked it up in the library. His chapel, in the garden, it reminded me of something. I searched through some books on ancient history, and his chapel isn't Roman, or Greek: it's Egyptian, from the time of the Pharaohs, the time of Moses. Those columns and paintings are just like what I saw in the book. He's crazy, he had an Egyptian temple built for himself in the garden. And the painted woman with cow horns on her head, I saw her in the book too, she's a goddess: Isis, or Cleopatra, like I saw in a movie."

"So, he's a pagan! I didn't think there were any left among white folk. What does he want to do with us in his temple?"

"I don't know. Maybe he wants to sketch our portrait, or photograph us, or film us. Maybe he wants to worship us. It's funny, don't you think?"

"You're as crazy as he is!"

"During the long vacation, whenever I have a little money, I go to the French Cultural Center to watch movies. I've always wished it were me in the movie, that I were an actress. So we're going to play goddesses at old whitey's place. It'll be just like in the movies."

"I'm coming with you, to protect you. I'll hide a little knife under my skirt to defend us. You never know."

The jeep was waiting behind the great Rutare rock. As soon as he saw the girls, Monsieur de Fontenaille greeted them with a grand wave of his bush hat. Veronica noticed that his shaven head shone like the glittering lake at the foot of the mountains. Then a cloud shrouded the sun, the lake stopped shimmering, and Monsieur de Fontenaille put his khaki hat back on.

"I've brought a friend," Veronica said, "just like I told you. This is Virginia."

Monsieur de Fontenaille scrutinized her for a long while.

"Hello, Virginia," he said at last. "Welcome. I shall call you Candace, Queen Candace."

Virginia had to restrain herself from bursting into laughter.

"I'm called Virginia, but my real name is Mutamuriza. Call me Candace if you like. The whites have always given us the names they wanted. Virginia, after all, is not one my father chose either."

"Let me explain. Candace isn't a white name, it's a queen's name, a black queen's name, the Queen of the Nile. And you Tutsi are her sons and daughters. Come on, hop in."

The jeep shot off, kicking up a shower of grass and mud, then zigzagged between the rocks, following an invisible track.

Veronica and Virginia clung to each other to avoid being thrown from the vehicle. They soon passed under the metal arch marking the entrance to the estate, snaked between the rambling coffee bushes and the row of identical maisonettes. "This was where my workers lived," Monsieur de Fontenaille explained, "back in the days when I thought coffee would make me rich. I was an imbecile but a good boss all the same. Now I house my herders, my warriors, and my *ingabo* in them. You'll see soon enough." The jeep stopped in front of the steps leading into the large villa.

They entered the living room, with its trophies, and were greeted by a military salute from the servant in white livery and golden epaulettes. Monsieur de Fontenaille motioned to the girls to sit down in the rattan armchairs, and the uniformed fellow placed glasses of orangeade on the coffee table, along with a tray of sweets.

Monsieur de Fontenaille sat opposite his guests on a sort of bamboo sofa draped with tattered leopard skins. He remained silent for quite a stretch, his head buried in his hands. Finally, his fingers slid down along his face, revealing eyes that shone with such brilliant intensity that Virginia hastened to check she still had the little knife beneath her skirt, while Veronica discreetly signaled to her that they should be prepared to flee. But Monsieur de Fontenaille didn't fling himself at them; instead, he began to speak.

He spoke for ages. At times, his voice trembled with emotion, at others it grew deep; sometimes it was no more than a whisper, before suddenly booming out again. He talked on and on about the great secret he would share with them, a secret that concerned them, the secret of the Tutsi. He explained that during their long exodus, the Tutsi had lost their Memory. They retained their cattle, their noble bearing, and their daughters' beauty, but they had lost their Memory. They no longer knew where they came from, or who they were. But he, Fontenaille, knew where the Tutsi came from, and who they were. How he came to know was a long story, the story of his life. It was his destiny, and he wasn't ashamed to say so.

Back in Europe, he had wanted to be a painter, but nobody bought his paintings, and his noble family – he sniggered as he pronounced the word – had long since lost all their money. So he set off for Africa to seek his fortune. He acquired some land, up here in the mountains, where nobody wanted to settle: a large estate where he could grow arabica coffee. He became a plantation owner, a colonist. He grew rich. He enjoyed going on safari in Kenya and Tanganyika. He kept an open house, and despite the impossible roads, guests coming up from the capital made sure not to miss a single one of his receptions, under any circumstances. They would gather in the large living room to drink a lot and talk a lot: the latest gossip from the capital, the animals they'd killed, coffee prices, the unfathomable stupidity of their servants, the natives one could never entirely enlighten, the girls accompanying the guests, or those their host obligingly provided – beautiful girls, Tutsi mainly. "My models," as Fontenaille explained, for he liked to sketch, painting herders leaning on their long sticks, lyre-horned cattle, young women balancing pointy baskets or jugs on their heads, pretty girls with their hair piled high and held in place by diadems of glass beads. He collected the portraits of those girls who agreed to enter the villa. Their faces fascinated him.

It was the tales told about the Tutsi that convinced him. That they weren't Negroes: one only had to look at their noses, and the reddish gleam of their skin. But where did they come from? The mystery of the Tutsi ate away at him. He'd gone and questioned the old bearded missionaries. He'd read everything there was to read on the subject. Nobody agreed on anything. One said the Tutsi came from Ethiopia, another that they were black Jews of some kind, or emigrant Copts from Alexandria, perhaps Romans who'd gotten lost, maybe cousins of the Fula or the Maasai, Sumerian survivors of Babylon, some even said they'd come all the way from Tibet, true Aryans. Fontenaille swore to himself that he'd find out the truth.

When the Hutu kicked out the head Mwami of Rwanda and began to massacre the Tutsi, with the help of the Belgians and the missionaries, he understood how urgent it was that he fulfill the promise he'd made to himself. It would now be his life's mission. The Tutsi would disappear, of that he was certain. Here they would eventually be exterminated, while those who had gone into exile would ensure their own people's decline through interbreeding. All that could be saved was the legend, the legend that was the truth. So he neglected his friends and abandoned the plantation. He learned to decipher hieroglyphs. He attempted to study Coptic and Ge'ez. He tried to speak Kinyarwanda with his servant. But he was clearly no scholar, or anthropologist, or ethnologist. All those books, all those studies, led nowhere. For he was an artist, intuition and inspiration were his only guides, and they took him much further than all these scholars with their erudition. So he decided to continue his research in the field, in Sudan and in Egypt. There he saw the goddess's temple before it was swallowed by the desert, and he saw the pyramids of the black pharaohs, the steles of the Candace queens by the Nile. That's where he found the proof he sought. Those faces carved in stone were the same as those he had sketched. All his doubts were gone. It was like an epiphany. The empire of the black pharaohs, that was exactly where the Tutsi came from. Chased off by Christianity, by Islam, by desert barbarians, they undertook the long trek to the source of the Nile, which they believed to be the land of the Gods who, by virtue of the river, bestowed plenty. They had kept their cows, their sacred bulls, and their noble bearing, their daughters had kept their beauty. But they had lost their Memory.

He, Fontenaille, was now going to fulfill his mission. He had abandoned everything for her. He had rebuilt the goddess's temple, and the pyramid of the black pharaohs. He had painted the goddess, and Candace, the queen. "And you," he said, "because you are beautiful, because you look like them, you will get your Memory back, thanks to me."

Monsieur de Fontenaille led them to his workshop. With some difficulty, they weaved their way through the stacks of boxes of drawings. There, on an easel, was a sketched portrait.

"But that's you, Veronica," said Virginia.

"Yes," said Monsieur de Fontenaille. "That is indeed our goddess, but you'll see her better in her temple."

The walls were hung with reproductions and photographs of frescoes, bas-reliefs, and steles depicting black pharaohs on their thrones; gods with falcon heads, jackal heads, crocodile heads; goddesses crowned with solar discs and cattle horns. Monsieur de Fontenaille paused before a large map of the River Nile. Veronica noticed that none of the place-names on it matched those she had read in her geography book.

"That's Philae, the temple of the Great Goddess," explained Monsieur de Fontenaille. "And there, that's Meroë, capital of the Kush, the empire of the black pharaohs, of the Candace; capital of a thousand pyramids. I've been there for you, the Tutsi, and I found you there. Here, I'll show you."

He handed her a sheet from one of the boxes.

"It's your portrait. I did it based on the rough sketches I made at the pilgrimage. And now I'll set it next to this photo I took at Meroë. It shows Isis, the Great Goddess, spreading her wings to protect the kingdom. Her breasts are bared. Look closely at her face, it's your own, to the last detail. Someone did your portrait in Meroë three thousand years ago. This proves it."

"But I wasn't around three thousand years ago, I don't have wings, and the kingdom is gone."

"Just wait and see, you'll soon understand. Now we must go to the temple."

"Veronica," said Monsieur de Fontenaille, "when you came to the temple for the first time, you probably didn't take in my fresco well. Look closely at the faces of the young women bringing offerings to the Great Goddess, don't you recognize some of them?"

"Oh, yes," said Virginia, "the third one there, that's me! And the one just in front of her is Emmanuella, who was in her final year a couple of years ago. And there's Brigitte, who's in tenth grade. It's like he's painted every Tutsi in the lycée."

"Well, I'm not there."

"You're not in the procession because you're the chosen one. Turn around and you'll see," said Monsieur de Fontenaille.

There on the back wall, the face of the Great Goddess was indeed that of Veronica. Only the eyes were strangely large.

"You see," said Monsieur de Fontenaille, "last Sunday, I had ample time to observe you closely. Then I corrected the face of the goddess so it really looks like yours. Now you can no longer deny it: you are Isis."

"I am no such thing. I don't like you making fun of me. And it's dangerous to mock the spirits of the dead. The *abazimu* might turn on you, and their vengeance is often cruel."

"Don't be upset. Soon you'll understand. Follow me, the tour's not over yet."

They exited the temple and climbed up to the ridge. A few long-horned cows were grazing on the slope, watched by young herders. On a nearby hill lay the enclosure where the cattle returned every evening. The dome of the main hut, with its artistically plaited tuft, rose above the encircling corral of shrubs. "See," said Monsieur de Fontenaille, "if the Tutsi were to disappear, I would at least save their cows, the *inyambo*. Perhaps it was a bull like that one there, a sacred bull, who led them as far as here." At the summit, in the midst of a thicket of old trees, like a slice of forest, stood a pyramid, taller and more tapering than the one erected by the Belgians at the source of the Nile. "That's where I made excavations," he explained. "The elders said it was the grave of a queen, Queen Nyiramavugo. So I ordered a dig and we found a skeleton, pearls, pottery, and copper bracelets. I'm no archaeologist. I didn't want the Queen's remains ending up in a museum, behind glass. So I had them fill in the trench and build this pyramid on top of it. Queen Nyiramavugo has a sepulcher befitting a Candace queen. Come here, Virginia, since from now on you, too, are queen, Queen Candace. Make whole the chain of time once again. Now everything is in place. The temple, the pyramid, the sacred bull. And I've rediscovered Isis and Candace, as beautiful as the day the world was formed. The ending will be as the beginning. That is the secret. Isis has returned to the spring. I have the secret, the secret, the se . . ."

Monsieur de Fontenaille seemed to be having great difficulty containing the exaltation that overwhelmed him, his hands shook, his throat was tight. To calm down, he went and sat on a rock a little way away, and spent a long while contemplating the rolling mountains that seemed to soar to infinity beneath the clouds.

"I don't think he even sees the same landscape as we do," said Veronica. "He probably fills it with goddesses, Candace queens, and black pharaohs. It's like a movie playing in his head, but now he wants flesh-and-blood actresses, and that's us."

"The Tutsi have already acted in white men's B movies, or in their craziness, you should say, and we suffered for it. I don't want to play Queen What's-Her-Name. I want to get back to the lycée. Come on, let's tell him to drive us back."

As the young women drew near, Monsieur de Fontenaille seemed to awaken from a deep sleep.

"The rain's coming," said Veronica. "It's late, you have to drive us back to the path."

"I'll take you. Don't worry, no one will see you. But next Sunday, I'll be waiting for you. It'll be the big day. Much better than the pilgrimage to Our Lady of the Nile."

It was Immaculée who found Veronica splayed at the bottom of the dormitory stairs.

"Help! Help! Veronica's dead, she fell, she's not moving."

The lycée girls had just sat down at the refectory tables, but they rushed over to the staircase. Virginia got there first and leaned over Veronica.

"Nonsense. She's not dead, she's not dead, she fainted, she fell down the stairs and banged her head on a step."

"Must've had one too many," said Gloriosa. "She must've gone to Leonidas's bar. She's scared of nothing, that girl. Shameless. The boys bought her a few drinks, and she didn't say no."

"Maybe she's been poisoned," said Immaculée. "There are way too many jealous girls in this place."

Sister Gertrude, who doubled as a nurse, fought her way through the throng of girls.

"Move back, give her some air. Help me carry her to the infirmary."

Sister Gertrude took Veronica's shoulders and Virginia lifted her legs, shoving a suddenly helpful Gloriosa out of the way: "Don't you dare touch her!"

They laid Veronica on the metal bed in the infirmary. Virginia wanted to stay and watch over her friend, but Sister Gertrude asked her to leave and shut the door. A small group of girls waited outside for the Sister's diagnosis. Sister Gertrude eventually opened the door and declared:

"It's nothing, just a bout of malaria, I'll deal with it. She mustn't be disturbed, there's nothing more for you to do here."

Sleep eluded Virginia. What had happened to Veronica? What had that madman de Fontenaille done to her? Virginia didn't dare imagine. The whites here thought they could do anything – they were white. Virginia reproached herself for refusing to accompany her friend. The two of them would have defended themselves; she had her little knife and would have convinced Veronica to flee before it was too late. As soon as the wake-up bell sounded, while the others washed and the Sisters attended morning Mass, Virginia slipped off to the infirmary. Veronica was sitting on the bed, her face deep in a large bowl. As soon as she saw her friend, she put the bowl down on the bedside table: "You see," she said. "Sister Gertrude's been taking good care of me, she gave me some milk."

"What happened to you? Tell me before Sister gets back."

"It's tricky, like waking from a bad dream, a nightmare. I don't know if what I'm about to tell you actually happened. The whites are worse than our poisoners. So I went to the meeting place, at the rock. The jeep was waiting for me, but it wasn't Fontenaille at the wheel. It was a young guy, a Tutsi obviously, probably one of those he calls his *ingabo*. In the living room was that servant with the gold braid, holding his tray of orange juice. He told me to drink it. The juice tasted funny. Fontenaille entered, draped in a white cloth with one shoulder bare.

"'Your friend didn't come?'

"'No, she's sick.'

"'Too bad, that's her loss, she won't discover her Truth.'

"I can't recall what happened to me next. It was like I had no more free will, like I no longer belonged to myself. There was something, someone, in me, stronger than me. I saw myself in the temple. I was like the painted women on the wall. I don't know who undressed me. My breasts were bare and I was wrapped in see-through gold fabric. But I felt no shame. It was like a dream you can't wake from, and I saw myself in this dream. Around me, the fresco warriors had stepped off the wall. They didn't really look like *intore*. All they wore were these cropped shorts, and they carried lances and large cowhide shields. I've no idea whether their hair had been straightened, or whether they were wearing wigs. Now I think they were the warriors Fontenaille was talking about. I felt like I was in a movie. Fontenaille made me sit on the throne and placed the hat with the large horns on my head. I saw him as if through a fog, sweeping his arms about and speaking incomprehensible words like the priest at Mass. I can't remember what occurred after that. I lost consciousness. Maybe I fell from the throne. I don't remember anything. When I came to my senses, I was in the jeep. It was the young servant who was driving. I was wearing my uniform again – someone must have put it on me. He dropped me very close to the lycée, telling me, 'Try to walk in without drawing attention. Take care of yourself, and not a word to anyone. But have a good look in your bra, there's bound to be something in there for you.' I managed to make my way upstairs. Inside my bra I found ten thousand-franc notes. I hid them in my suitcase. But as I came back down, everything started to spin, and I fell."

"And he didn't do anything to you?"

"No, he didn't touch me. He's not like the other whites, who only want to fling you into bed. What he wants is to play out his crazy notions. I'm his Isis."

"Why did he drug you, then?"

"I don't know. He was afraid I would refuse to play along, that I'd make fun of him. He wanted everything to happen exactly as he had dreamed, so he made me drink his potion, but he overdid it, he's a bad poisoner. There are limits to my curiosity, after all, do you think I'd have agreed to go along with his ridiculous game without his potion? There was a letter with the banknotes. He said that he was sorry he had to make me drink his potion, and for not trusting me, but he had no choice: there was no room for failure. He hopes I'll understand and that I'll still come back and see him. I'm the only one who can play goddess. He's invited me to stay at his place during the long vacation. He'll pay my fees, even for me to go to Europe. He's prepared to spend a lot of money on this . . ."

"And you believe his promises?"

"Can you imagine if they were true?"

"You're as crazy as he is. You'll end up believing you're the goddess. You know what happened to us Tutsi when some agreed to play the role the whites assigned to us. My grandmother told me how when the whites arrived, they thought we were dressed like savages. They sold glass beads, loads of pearls, and tons of white cloth to the women, the chiefs' wives. They showed them how to wear it all and how to fix their hair. They turned them into the Ethiopians, the Egyptians they'd come all this way to seek. Now they had their proof. They dressed them to fit their own delusions."

The Blood of Shame

Once again she was woken up by that same bad dream. Her schoolmates were furious; they made fun of her, for she let out a cry loud enough to wake them, too. It happened much too often. They were going to complain to the dorm monitor.

Modesta was no longer sure whether it had really been a nightmare. She looked at the sheets. Then, still in bed, she lifted her nightdress and felt between her thighs. No, there was nothing. It was just a bad dream that had plagued her ever since she became a woman. Perhaps it was a curse or an evil spell that someone had cast on her, someone she didn't know, a hidden enemy, maybe a person very close to her, one of her schoolmates. Or else it came from farther away, from back home, a jealous neighbor; she had no idea, perhaps she never would.

In the dream, she was sometimes in her own bed, but more often in class. She began to bleed, a huge red patch soaking into her blue dress, sticky blood between her thighs, and down her legs, a long stream flowing under her seat and beneath the other desks. The pupils started screaming: "It's her again, she's bleeding, she's bleeding . . . It'll never end!" And the teacher shouted: "We must take her to Sister Gerda. She knows what to do with girls who bleed anywhere and everywhere." And suddenly she found herself in Sister Gerda's office, with an angry Sister Gerda shouting at her: "Look at that! It's what I've always said: that's what it means to be a woman. And you all want to become women. It's your own fault! And now there's all that blood. It's never ending!"

Modesta didn't like to remember. And yet the same memory kept flooding back. It was no longer a dream, more a memory she kept reliving, like a sin she'd never be able to atone for. It began the year she started middle school. She had passed the national exam and was therefore able to join the core curriculum. She felt proud. Her parents felt proud. The neighbors felt proud, and jealous. She felt proud that her neighbors felt jealous because of her. They went to the tailor's to have her uniform made; they purchased exercise books and pens from the Saint-Michel Économat; from a Pakistani shop in Muhima, they bought material to make two sheets. The list also specified two meters of white fabric, the type known as *americani*. She had no idea what that could be for.

Neither did her father. She didn't ask her mother, who knew nothing about school stuff. She hadn't dared ask the parish priest. They put everything into the suitcase they'd bought specially for her, since her big sister's case was too battered. She needed a new case to make a good impression, for the sake of her family's honor. When they got to school, the sister monitor checked the contents. It was all there, including the *americani* material, which the sister appeared to consider especially important: "You're to bring it along to the first sewing lesson," she told her.

The sixth-grade class soon split into two cliques: those with breasts, and those without. Those with breasts began to scorn those without. They chatted a lot with the older girls, all of whom had breasts. It was as if they had secrets to share. Modesta was one of those without breasts. Yet she had two little nipples, budding breasts, that gave some contour to her chest. But for reasons Modesta couldn't fathom, the older girls hadn't wanted her to join their faction.

In the first sewing class, two days after the start of the school year, the teacher checked they all had their *americani*. Modesta showed her length of fabric, along with the other girls. "We're going to make strips," she said, "that's our very first task. Everyone must have finished by the end of class." The teacher handed out scissors and patterns, and the pupils cut the material into long strips, and then each strip into twenty sections. "Now, fold the twenty pieces in four, then sew the edges. Each piece should look like a little mattress." Next, she had them make a string-drawn bag, into which they put the twenty strips. "Those who don't need them yet, pack them carefully in your suitcase for now."

But there were many more mysteries. In the garden, behind a bamboo grove, stood a small brick house surrounded by a low wall. "That's the purdah house," said the older ones, laughing, "and you breastless young girls have no business there; don't you even come close." But for the Sisters, it was no laughing matter. There was always one of them keeping watch on the forbidden house, chasing away any servants or gardeners who approached it, and handing out severe punishments to the younger girls who hung around nearby out of curiosity. This sentry duty was mostly performed by Sister Gerda, the Keeper of the Mystery. She became quite fierce if she caught any of the little ones trying to follow any Initiates of the Mysteries as they walked toward the forbidden place carrying a bucket. But deep down, the girls without breasts knew very well that all these mysteries – the *americani* strips, the "dirty den," the bucket – would soon be revealed to them. They knew their turn would come.

Initiation: the fear, the shame. For Modesta, it happened in class. During English. She felt a warm liquid running down her legs, and when she stood up, her classmates in the row behind saw a large red stain spreading across her dress, and blood dripping onto the cement floor. "Madame!" cried the girl sitting next to Modesta, as she pointed at her. The teacher saw the puddle of blood. "Quick," she said, "Immaculée, take her to Sister Gerda." Modesta followed Immaculée, weeping floods of tears. "Don't cry," said Immaculée, "it happens to every girl. Surely you didn't expect to escape it. You're a real woman now. You'll have children." Immaculée knocked at the door of Sister Gerda's office. "Well, well," said Sister Gerda, "here's Modesta, I wasn't expecting it so soon. So, we're a young woman now. You'll see how much you have to suffer for that: it's God's will, payment for Eve's sin; Eve, who opened the door to the devil; Eve, the mother of us all. Women are made to suffer. Modesta, what a beautiful name for a woman, for a Christian woman. From now on, every month, this blood will remind you that you're only a woman, and if ever you float off thinking you're beautiful, it will be there to remind you of what you are: just a woman."

After Modesta took a shower, Sister Gerda initiated her into the Mysteries of a woman's cycles. She showed her how to use the strips she now called "sanitary pads." She told her to go to the school shop and buy a little bucket with a lid in which to put the used pads, as well as a slab of household soap. There'd be no need to explain why to Sister Bernadette behind the counter.

Sister Gerda asked for the key to the dormitory, which remained shut all day, opened the doors wide so that Modesta could get a pad from the bag, and then took Modesta to the little brick house. As soon as she opened the door, the acrid, fetid stench made Modesta step back. "Go on in," said Sister Gerda, "You can't go back now, it's too late to pretend you're still a girl." Inside the shadowy room, lit only by a narrow wire-mesh window, Modesta saw washing lines stretched from one wall to another, from which dangled sanitary pads in shades of pink, gray, purplish-blue, and dirty white, that the boarders had hung out to dry. "At the back," said Sister Gerda, "there's a tub for you to wash your dirty pads. You'll scrub and you'll scrub, but you'll never scrub hard enough to erase the sin of being a woman. And believe me, I could tell you the owner of each and every pad, those who scrub and those who don't. You can spot the lazy ones immediately: their pads remain steeped in their menstrual secretions. Shame on them! So make sure you scrub, Modesta, to avoid piling shame upon shame."

Modesta liked to confide in Virginia, sharing her secrets in private, well away from prying eyes, especially those of Gloriosa. Yes, a Hutu girl could be friends with a Tutsi girl. It didn't impose any future obligations upon them. Whenever it would finally prove necessary for the majority people to become the majority for good, Hutu girls would know full well which race they belonged to. Because there were two races in Rwanda. Or three. The whites had said so; they were the ones who had discovered it. They'd written about it in their books. Experts came from miles around and measured all the skulls. Their conclusions were irrefutable. Two races: Hutu and Tutsi, also known as Bantu and Hamite.

The third race wasn't even worth mentioning. But Modesta wasn't fully Hutu. Of course she was considered Hutu because her father was. And it's the father who matters. But because of her mother, you could say that she was only half Hutu – and indeed many did say that. It was dangerous for her to be seen hanging around with a Tutsi girl. People would immediately ask her: "So, which side are you on? Do you really know who you are? You must be a traitor, a spy for those *inyenzi* – cockroaches. You pass yourself off as a Hutu, but really you gravitate toward the Tutsi whenever you can, because you consider them your real family.'

But there was worse. The suspicions surrounding Modesta were not only because of her mother. After all, many Hutu leaders had taken Tutsi wives. Trophies of their victory. Wasn't the President's wife Tutsi? No, what made Modesta's situation even worse was her father, Rutetereza, the Hutu who had wanted to become a Tutsi – *kwihutura* they called it, to "de-Hutufy" oneself. He did indeed have some of the physical attributes associated with Tutsi, he was very tall, with a short nose and a wide forehead, but he was actually one of those many Rwandans referred to as *ikijakazi* – "neither one nor the other." He came from a good Hutu family, and spent a few years as a seminary student before becoming secretary, accountant, and steward to a Tutsi chief, of whom he became fond, emulating him and his ways. He grew rich from discreetly, yet diligently, siphoning off some of the taxes he collected on behalf of his boss. He bought cattle. And to show off his new wealth, he gave a cow to a Tutsi neighbor who had lost his own herd. He wanted to hear him exclaim the customary appreciation: "Rutetereza! You who gave me a cow! *Yampaye inka Rutetereza!*" To complete his metamorphosis, he decided to marry a Tutsi. A poor Tutsi family gave him one of their daughters. One beautiful daughter, in exchange for a cow. His boss had become one of the most conservative leaders of the Tutsi party, and he wanted to follow suit. "Rutetereza," said his boss, "you've done all you can, but you're still not Tutsi. Stay with your own people." So he campaigned for a Hutu party that wanted the King to remain in power. But the Parmehutu Party won and the Republic was proclaimed. Nobody gave him any trouble, since he came from a good Hutu family, and had enjoyed the protection of some of his brothers who had fought for the winning Party. But he couldn't secure any of the important positions, he'd always be a minor civil servant, and there would always be someone to remind him how he'd wanted to turn Tutsi, *kwihutura*. He would never be free of the jokes, or threats (there was little difference), from those who liked to remind him of his treachery. So he stuffed them with grilled goat and beans, and sloshed them with banana beer and Primus, for that was the price of *kwitutsura*, of "de-Tutsifying" himself, becoming Hutu again. The same cloud of suspicion hung over Modesta. She had to keep reminding the others that she was a real Hutu, especially Gloriosa, whose name resounded like a slogan: Nyiramasuka, "She of the Hoe." Modesta had to be Gloriosa's best friend.

Nevertheless, and for reasons she didn't grasp, something pushed her to divulge her secrets to Virginia, her deepest secrets, the ones she couldn't reveal to anyone else. She eventually told her about her nightmares, about the menstrual blood that haunted her dreams. Virginia said nothing at first. She didn't know what to say. There are many things that are never discussed in Rwanda, and that is one of them. But she was touched by Modesta's willingness to confide in her. Could she really be her friend? Today, she was. But tomorrow? She, too, began to tell Modesta about her periods. It felt a bit scary to talk about something that was never supposed to be mentioned, but this flow of forbidden words was like a release for her. Yes, in that moment, Modesta was truly her friend.

"You know quite well we're not to talk about that. Little girls don't have a clue what's happening to them. They think they're cursed. I don't know if it was like that before the Europeans came, but the missionaries only made matters worse. Our mothers stay silent, it's taboo, as the teachers would say. It's always got to be your big sister or a friend who explains it, and reassures you as best she can. That's what it was like, up on my hill; perhaps it was different in town. My best friend was Speciosa. She didn't pass the national exam, so she remained in the village. Throughout primary school, we were inseparable. We had so much fun, as much as the boys did. Sure, we helped our mothers in the fields and carried our baby brothers on our backs, we were already little moms. But what we liked best was going to the lake to do laundry. Not like the huge lake you can see from up here every now and then. No, a small lake at the foot of my hill.

"During the long vacation, in the dry season, off we go, all the girls who live on the hill, older girls on one side, younger ones on the other. There's just two or three brainy girls who don't feel like joining us; they say they've got a meeting with some other students, or that they've got choir practice at the mission. We just ignore and tease them. The shore of the lake bristles with reeds and papyrus sedge, except where we draw water and do the laundry. Still, you've got to be careful: if a fallen tree trunk lying on the sand starts to shift, that's a crocodile. We spend the whole afternoon washing and beating the laundry, then we spread it on the grass, which is always green, even during the dry season. Once that's done, we undress and rush into the water, splashing each other, and rubbing each other's backs. It's quite unlike the lycée showers – they're so sad. Then we go into the papyrus sedge to dry off. We stay there, naked, hidden in the papyrus, watching passersby. We make fun of them . . .

"But one day, during the long vacation (I was in the sixth grade), I went to fetch Speciosa just like I did every morning. She wasn't waiting for me at the entrance to the enclosure. I saw her mother running toward me, her arms in the air. 'Don't come in,' she said. 'You can't see Speciosa, no one can see Speciosa at the moment.' I didn't understand. What contagious disease could Speciosa have caught? I insisted. I asked her, again and again: 'Speciosa's my friend, why can't I see her?' Finally, she gave in, saying that in any case what was happening to Speciosa would soon happen to me. I stepped inside the house. Speciosa lay on her bed. Under her was a fresh layer of straw. When she saw me, she started to cry. Then she sat up. I saw the grass all soaked with blood. 'Look,' she said. 'That's my blood. It's how you become a woman. Every month I'll be shut up in my room. Mommy told me that's how it is for women. She takes the straw I've soiled, and at night she burns it, secretly. Then she buries the ashes in a deep hole. She's scared a witch doctor might steal it for his evil spells, and our fields will wither, and my sisters and I will become infertile because of my first menstrual blood that could put the whole family at risk. We won't be able to play like before. Now I'm a woman, with a woman's wraparound, and I feel really miserable.' We never played together after that."

"It was just like that for me, too. My first period came when I was at school. But before that, at home, I didn't understand why my mother kept an eye on my chest. You know, out in the countryside, all we wear is a small piece of fabric as a skirt. It's the only garment that little girls wear. We're like boys. We all play together. When I turned ten, my mother and her neighbors started to spy on me. Their gaze was focused on my chest when I danced. And as soon as my mother noticed there were these little buds sprouting, she told me to cover them up, and not to show them to any men, not even my father. She gave me one of my brother's old shirts, showed me how to sit, and especially how to lower my eyes when people spoke to me. 'It's only girls with no shame, and the broad-minded women of Kigali, who look a man in the face,' she used to tell me. It must've been the same for you. But now we should be delighted at the sight of blood every month. It means we're women, real women who'll have children. You know very well that we must bear children in order to become real women. When they marry you off, that's what they expect of you. You're nothing to your new family, or to your husband, if you don't have children. You must have children, boys, above all boys. It's when you bear sons that you become a real woman, a mother, worthy of respect."

"Of course I want children like everyone else. But I want my children to be neither Hutu nor Tutsi. Neither half-Hutu nor half-Tutsi. I just want them to be mine, that's all. Sometimes, I tell myself it would be better if I didn't have children. I'm thinking of becoming a nun like Sister Lydwine. With their veils and long dresses, I get the feeling that the Sisters are no longer women like us. Have you noticed they don't have breasts? I imagine that when you're a nun, you don't have periods either. What would be the point?"

"Well, I'm sure Sisters have periods just like every woman. I've got a cousin who's with the Benebikira Sisters. She told me they also hand out sanitary pads, just like we get."

"All I know is that I don't want to turn into my mother, and be treated the way she's treated. Ever since my father became a Hutu again, he's ashamed of her. He hides her. She can no longer leave the house. It's no longer she who serves beer to my father's friends, those who still come visit. He calls for my little sisters. She's lucky if he lets her go to Sunday Mass: early Mass, not High Mass. He's even tried to find her a great-great-great Hutu grandfather, a Hutu chief, an *umuhinza*. Everyone had a good laugh when he came out with that. My older brothers hate their mother, it's because of her they're not like everyone else, that people call them mulattos or Hutsi. Jean-Damascène, who's a solider, says it's because of her that he'll always remain a lieutenant, because they'll never trust him. I'm the only one who still speaks to her, kind of in secret, like with you. As far as I'm concerned, she's neither Hutu nor Tutsi, she's my mother."

"Maybe one day, there'll be a Rwanda with neither Hutu nor Tutsi."

"Maybe. Hey, watch out, there's Gloriosa; hope she didn't see us together."

"Quick, go and be with your best friend, Modesta, off you go . . ."

The Gorillas

There were two things that set Monsieur de Decker apart from the other teachers. The first was that he was the only one with a wife. The others were either single – the young Frenchmen, for example – or else they had left their wives behind in Europe, although perhaps their spouses had simply refused to follow them into these remote mountains. In some sense, Madame de Decker was the only true white woman at the lycée of Our Lady of the Nile, since Mother Superior and Sister Bursar were not entirely women, nor entirely white: they were nuns. They couldn't marry, they would never have children, they no longer had breasts. They'd lived so long in Rwanda that their color had been quite forgotten. They were hybrid creatures – neither men nor women, neither black nor white – that Rwandans had grown used to, just as they had grown used to the landscape of coffee plantations and cassava fields the Belgians had forced them to plant under their rule. As for Miss South, she must've been a woman but she wasn't white, but red, and she was English.

Monsieur de Decker's wife didn't always live with her husband in the bungalow. She spent long spells in Kigali, but one always knew when she was here, because the laundry servant would hang Madame's clothes under the awning behind the villa. The lycée girls hovered around the bungalow to admire Madame de Decker's wardrobe. They were astonished at the number of dresses hanging there, counting and comparing them; some even tried to fix in their memory the design they liked most, so they could get the tailor to copy it. Madame de Decker's arrival at the lycée was always highly anticipated, and the subject of fierce discussion. The girls were relieved to finally see a real white woman at Our Lady of the Nile, and the proof: Madame de Decker was blond.

Monsieur de Decker's other particularity was his lessons. He was our natural science teacher, and his class was quite the Noah's Ark – every animal on the planet paraded through it. He projected slides onto a white sheet pinned to the blackboard, without much in the way of commentary, showing us the Peruvian llama, the Tibetan yak, the Arctic polar bear, the Friesian cow, the Saharan dromedary, the Mexican jaguar, the Ngorongoro rhinoceros, the Camargue bull, the Indian tiger, the Chinese panda, and the Australian kangaroo. Then came that great day, at the end of the first term, when Monsieur de Decker showed us his own photos, those he had taken up in the bamboo forest, beyond the clouds, on the slopes of the volcanoes, almost at risk to his own life: pictures of gorillas. When it came to gorillas, you could never get him to shut up. Monsieur de Decker was the one and only expert. Much to his wife's despair, he climbed Mount Muhabura every weekend to observe them; this year, he had even sacrificed his trip back to Belgium for the long vacation. It was as if he'd always lived in their midst. He was most at ease with the dominant male who had let him count his females. A mother gorilla whose young he'd tended remained duly grateful. However much the guides might caution prudence, try to hold him back, Monsieur de Decker had no fear of these great apes. He was familiar with the character of each member of the group, could predict their reactions, and was able to communicate with them. Indeed, he no longer even needed a guide. The gorillas, he felt certain, were Rwanda's future, her treasure, her opportunity. They needed protecting and their habitat needed to be expanded. The whole world had entrusted Rwanda with a sacred mission: to save the gorillas!

Monsieur de Decker's pronouncements on the gorillas drove Goretti to a fury.

"What!" she exploded. "Again it's the *whites* who discovered gorillas, just as they discovered Rwanda, Africa, and the whole planet! What about us Bakiga, haven't the gorillas always been our neighbors? And our Batwa, were they afraid of the gorillas when they hunted them with their little bows and arrows? You'd think the gorillas only belong to the Bazungu now. They're the only ones who can see them, or get close to them. They're in love with the gorillas. The only interesting thing in Rwanda are the gorillas. All Rwandans must be at the service of the gorillas, tending to their every need, caring only for the gorillas, making them the entire focus of their lives. There's even a white woman living among them. She hates all humans, especially Rwandans. She lives with the monkeys all year round. She built her home among the gorillas. She opened a health center for them. All the whites admire her. She receives a lot of money for the gorillas. I don't want to leave the gorillas to the whites. They're Rwandans too. We can't leave them to foreigners. It's my duty to go and see them. And I'll go. The teachers say the monkeys are our ancestors. That enrages Father Herménégilde. It's not what my mother says. According to her, the gorillas were once people who fled to the forest, she doesn't know why, and forgot to be humans. They spent so long in the forest they turned into hairy giants, but when they glimpse a young virgin, they remember how they were once human and try to abduct her, but the females, their legitimate and naturally jealous mates, prevent them by force."

"I saw that at the movies," Veronica interrupted, "a huge monkey holding a woman in his hand . . ."

"I'm not talking about something in the movies. I heard it

straight from my mother. Anyway, I must go visit the gorillas. We can't leave them to the whites; even a white woman who lives only for them. Does anyone want to come with me? We'll go during Christmas break. I'm sure my father will help me. Who wants to come along?"

They all turned to Gloriosa for her reaction, but she just shrugged her shoulders, burst out laughing, and muttered a few inaudible words, clearly unflattering to the Bakiga. The surprise came from Immaculée:

"I'll go with you if I can. If my dad gives me permission, count me in."

Gloriosa glowered at Immaculée for having just betrayed her in front of the whole class.

"I've had enough of cruising around with my boyfriend on his bike," said Immaculée. "I want something more exciting; then at least I'll have something to tell him: I'll be a girl who's scared of nothing, I'll be an adventurer!"

At the start of the January term, Goretti and Immaculée's inevitable account of their adventures on Gorilla Mountain was eagerly awaited. The "explorers," as Gloriosa mockingly referred to them, played the reluctant celebrities, saying little. "They got no farther than Ruhengeri," jeered Gloriosa, "drinking Primus and eating grilled chicken while gazing at far-off Mount Muhabura in the clouds." But one night after dinner, Goretti invited the whole class up to her room to hear the tale.

"So, did you see the gorillas?"

"You bet we saw them. We even touched them, or nearly. My father helped us, even though he's very busy at the moment: there's a lot of people who come see him at Ruhengeri military base; even Immaculée's dad, who drove us to Ruhengeri, he needed to speak to my dad . . . So my father gave orders for us to be kitted out: a jeep, four soldiers, provisions. We wore camouflage gear, and the soldiers laughed so much when they saw Immaculée in high heels that they gave us these huge combat boots same as they've got: you'll see in the photos.

"Anyway, we left at dawn, driving up the volcano in the jeep until we reached the forest. That's where we were supposed to meet the guides, but they weren't there. We spent ages waiting for them. The soldiers put two tents up: one for them, one for us. Finally, the head guide turned up, looking rather embarrassed. He said: 'Madame, the white woman doesn't want her gorillas disturbed. She says they don't like Rwandans, that they're frightened of them. They know it's the Rwandans who kill them. It's only whites who know how to handle them. That's what my boss says. So I can't take you there, or she'd fire me, and I don't want to lose my pay: I can already imagine my wife yelling. I can't stop you going any farther, but I won't be your guide.' He scampered off as fast as he could.

"We were heartbroken at the white woman's forbidding us to visit our gorillas. Then one of the soldiers spoke to the sergeant. And the sergeant came and told us that maybe there was a way we could still go see our gorillas. The solider knew the Batwa, and where their camp was. If we gave them something, they would certainly agree to guide us to the gorillas. We got back in the jeep and drove deep into the forest, following the soldier. The Batwa fled when they saw us coming. But the soldiers caught an old fellow who couldn't run as fast as the others. He was shaking, the poor old man. Immaculée and I tried to reassure him. I told him who I was and what we wanted. Luckily, I speak Kinyarwanda like they speak in Bukiga – you shouldn't tease me about it so much. When at last the old guy understood we just wanted to see the gorillas, he called the others back and we started to negotiate. It took forever. But I am, after all, the daughter of the colonel who runs the military base. And there were the four soldiers clutching their rifles. We eventually made a deal. Two goats. One goat before we set off, which we entrusted to the women, and a second goat once they had taken us to the gorillas. We returned to our tents. The sergeant left in the jeep to go buy two goats at the nearest market.

"We slept in the tent, like real soldiers. The next morning, the Batwa were back. They asked:

" 'Where are the goats?'

" 'Look,' said the sergeant.

"They examined them, and held a long discussion among themselves. The man who seemed to be the chief said he wanted to eat one straightaway, before taking us to the gorillas. The sergeant said it wasn't possible, that he was expected back at camp the following morning, they must head off to see the gorillas right away. The Batwa were having none of it, they wanted to eat one of the goats before setting off, plus they'd told their women and children to go collect firewood. The sergeant said it was the colonel who had given orders to take his daughter up to the gorillas because she wanted to see them. The Mutwa turned to me and began laughing. 'Now it's black women too who want to see the gorillas!' So I suggested that if they took us to see the gorillas immediately, I'd give them a third goat.

"'Fine, we'll go,' the chief said finally. 'I believe you really are the colonel's daughter, but don't forget, you're the one who's promised us a third goat. May lightning strike you down if we don't get it!'

"We walked deeper into the forest. There was no trail. The Batwa hacked a way through for us with their machetes. 'Paths,' they said, 'are for the Bazungu. Us, we're sons of the forest. Can a mother lose her children?' We walked for two hours, maybe three, I don't recall. The Batwa forged ahead, without looking back to see if we were following. We stumbled at every step, branches and lianas whipping at our faces. Even the soldiers were anxious, scared that the Batwa were leading them into some kind of ambush.

"Suddenly, the Batwa chief crouched down and motioned that we should do the same. He made a strange sound with his lips, then picked up a little stem of bamboo that he waved as if in greeting. And there, through the trees, we spotted them: roughly a dozen gorillas, I didn't count properly, with the biggest one, the head of the family, looking in our direction.

"'Heads down,' a Mutwa mumbled. 'Don't look at him, show him he's boss, that you submit to him, I don't think he likes your smell.'

"I buried my nose in the soil the way the Swahili of Nyami-rambo do when they pray. The great gorilla stood and uttered a growl. He was absolutely huge. 'It's okay,' said the Mutwa. 'He recognized me, he's satisfied, but don't move.'

"Still, I raised my head, and had time to get a good look at them: the big boss still on his guard, the females, and the little ones. Immaculée, am I lying? Didn't we see them really close up? Close enough to touch them."

"Sure we saw them. The mommy gorillas sat in a circle while the head of the family kept an eye on us. The little ones played and frolicked in the middle, spinning round and round, went to suckle at their mother's breast, got the fleas picked off them. The mommies chewed bamboo shoots for their young to eat, like our grandmothers did with sorghum. Then I thought about what Goretti's mother said: that gorillas were once humans. Well, let me suggest a different story: gorillas refused to become humans; they were almost humans but they preferred to remain monkeys in their forest atop the volcanoes. When they saw that other monkeys like them had become humans, but had also become mean and cruel and spent their time killing each other, they refused to become humans. Maybe that's the original sin Father Herméné-gilde is always talking about: when monkeys turned into men!"

"Immaculée, the philosopher!" sneered Gloriosa. "Miss Rwanda gets all theological! That's hilarious. Now we've heard it all. You should put that in your next essay, Father Herménégilde will be fascinated!"

"And then," Goretti continued, ignoring Gloriosa's sarcasm, "the Batwa motioned that we should leave without a sound. They said that the large male was getting annoyed. I think they were also eager to go and eat their goats. We returned to the camp. The third goat was fetched, the Batwa composed a song in honor of the three goats, and we made our way back to the military base. The officers congratulated us for being so daring: it's not just white women who are able to go visit the gorillas."

The whole audience clapped as the two "explorers" finished their tale.

"But, you say there were a lot of people at the military base, do you know why?" asked Gloriosa. "And you, Immaculée, what was your father doing in Ruhengeri, with the Bakiga?"

"He went to buy potatoes," replied Immaculée. "He's only interested in those fat Ruhengeri potatoes, the *intofanyi* type. He's had enough of those little ones from Gitarama or Banyan-duga, they disgust him."

Up the Virgin's Sleeve

"Father Herménégilde is charity personified," said Mother Superior when she introduced the chaplain and teacher of religion to visitors. "If only you knew how much time he devotes to ensuring the poor of the district are decently clothed, and that's in addition to all his spiritual and material responsibilities and duties!" Indeed, Father Herménégilde was the Catholic Relief Services' man in Nyaminombe. Every month, a truck from the humanitarian organization delivered fat bundles of old clothes, which the lycée hands stacked in a shed grudgingly provided by Brother Auxile for the chaplain's charitable works. No one understood why the CRS stamped on the tarpaulin covering the trucks made the French teachers laugh so much. Some of the garments went to Father Angelo, who redistributed them around the parish and farther afield; others were sold on to secondhand clothes dealers at the market, the proceeds then used to purchase blue and khaki material to make uniforms for children attending Nyaminombe's primary schools. Father Herménégilde kept a few garments, dresses mainly, for his own personal good works.

Father Herménégilde solicited the help of the lycée girls to sort the clothes, aiming his request at the new tenth graders, who, at the start of the school year, were still agog at the brave new world of the lycée they were only just discovering. "Show us how kind you are," he preached. "You who are the country's female elite, it is your duty to labor in support of the development of the peasant masses. Help me clothe those who are naked." The pupils felt obliged to show up at the shed door on Saturday afternoons, and few dared shirk their duty. After thanking them at length for such goodwill, Father Herménégilde chose from among the volunteers, with a predilection for Tutsi girls, and others with particularly pleasing physiques. Then there were a few old hands from previous years, who assessed the new recruits with a mixture of irony and disdain. The work entailed sorting the crumpled clothes into piles: one for kids, one for women, one for men. Nobody knew what to do with the down-lined jackets, padded coats, and caps with earflaps. "The old folk will take those," said Father Herménégilde. "They're always cold." From the pile of women's wear he picked out the most beautiful dresses, the finest blouses, and even the odd item of lacy underwear, all for his "own good works, and to reward you with," he promised, as encouragement to his troop of helpers.

Father Herménégilde gave out these rewards in his study, which doubled as his bedroom. Veronica was one of the first to receive such a reward, when she was in tenth grade. Father Herménégilde kept her back at the end of religion class. Once all the pupils had left, he told her: "I noticed you worked particularly hard last Saturday. That deserves a reward. Come see me tonight in my study after refectory. I've put something aside for you." Veronica sensed that there was nothing good about this "reward." The older girls would sometimes talk about it under their breath, mocking or expressing their outrage at those who'd received rewards, particularly those who went to collect one too often. There was nobody Veronica could turn to for advice, and anyway, she knew very well that being Tutsi, it would have been too reckless of her not to go and receive the "reward" Father Herménégilde had promised her.

Leaving the refectory, she tried to go upstairs to the first floor without being seen, and there, at the end of the corridor, was Father Herménégilde's study. She felt as if she was being watched by all the other girls, who would be bound to notice her absence at study time anyway. She knocked at the study door as discreetly as she could.

"Quick, come in," answered a voice with a kindness that surprised her.

Father Herménégilde sat behind a great black desk, on which stood an ivory Christ on the Cross, papers scattered across it – perhaps rough drafts of his lessons or sermons, thought Veronica. Behind him, beneath photos of the President and the Pope, the statue of Our Lady of Lourdes, repainted in the colors of Our Lady of the Nile, presided over bulging shelves of books and folders. To the right, a black curtain closed off an alcove, doubtless where the chaplain's bed lay.

"I've asked you here," Father Herménégilde said to her, "because you're very deserving of a reward. I've observed you closely and I appreciate the way you work. Of course you're a Tutsi, but all the same, I think you're a beautiful . . . a good girl. Take a look at the armchair beside you, I've picked out a pretty dress for you."

Spread out on one of the armchairs reserved for visitors was a pink dress with a lace décolleté. Veronica had no idea what to do or say, and she didn't dare approach the chair and the dress.

"It's for you, it's for you, don't be frightened," Father Herménégilde insisted. "But first I want to make sure it fits you, that it's your size, so you'll have to try it on, here, in front of me. I want to be sure it fits you properly, otherwise, I'll fetch you another one."

Father Herménégilde got up, came round the desk, took the dress and handed it to Veronica. She made to slip it over her uniform as Rwandan modesty requires.

"No, no, no," said Father Herménégilde, snatching back the frock, "that's not the way to try on such a lovely dress. I want to be sure it's a perfect fit, and to do that you must take off your uniform, that's how you try on a lovely dress like this."

"But Father, Father . . ."

"Do as I say. What's there to fear while you're with me? Have you forgotten I'm a priest? A priest's eyes know not concupiscence. It's as if they didn't see you. And you won't even be fully naked . . . not quite . . . not yet. Get on with it," he said irritably. "Don't forget who you are. You want to stay at the lycée, don't you? I could always . . . Take that uniform off, quickly."

Veronica let her blue uniform dress slip to her feet, leaving her standing in nothing but her bra and panties under the gaze of Father Herménégilde, who seemed in no rush to hand her the "reward." He went and sat in the armchair and contemplated her for a long while.

"Father, Father . . ." Veronica implored.

At last Father Herménégilde rose, came up to her, very close, gave her the pink dress, and with the pretext of zipping her up in the back, unclipped her bra.

"It's better like that," he murmured, "for the neckline, it's much better."

He stepped back a bit and then went to sit down in his chair.

"It's a little big, of course," he said, holding the uniform dress and the bra on his lap, "but it will do, all the same. Next time, I'll find one that fits you perfectly. Take the dress off and put your uniform back on."

Veronica waited for ages, arms crossed over her chest, until Father Herménégilde gave her back the blue dress and the bra.

"Back to your friends now, quickly. Don't say anything, or show the dress, they'll be jealous. You came for confession, that's all you need to say. But I don't like those cotton panties of yours. Next time, I'll bring you some lacy ones."

Never again was Veronica rewarded by Father Herménégilde. Frida took her place. She asked for a pair of lace panties the very first evening. The rest took place behind the black curtain.

Frida remained Father Herménégilde's appointed favorite for a whole year, which didn't stop the chaplain handing out "rewards" to other deserving and obliging pupils. But the next year, Frida's ambitions lay elsewhere. She spent her holidays in Kinshasa, where her father was First Secretary at the embassy. He viewed his daughter as a prime ornament for embassy dinners and receptions. Kinshasa likes to party through the night, and Frida was quite a hit on the dance floor. Her light skin, opulent grace, and shapely curves were just what Zairians liked, while the fact she was Rwandan added a touch of exoticism. So no one hid their surprise when it transpired that the affections of the daughter of the Rwandan Embassy's First Secretary had fallen upon a short, older man. It's true that Jean-Baptiste Balimba still went in for the Zairian *sapeur* look of tailored jacket, bell-bottoms, and flamboyant vest. It's also true he was rich, and in with President Mobutu's crowd, so they said. Frida's father openly encouraged his daughter's liaison, considering that it could only be good for his diplomatic career. They even held a party to celebrate their unofficial engagement while awaiting the outcome of putative wedding negotiations. Of course it was rumored that Jean-Baptiste Balimba had other wives dotted along the length of the River Zaire (formally Congo) as far as Katanga (now known as Shaba). Well might her father worry that his daughter Frida would become "yet another posting." And a posting only lasts a certain time. To prove his sincerity, Balimba requested he be appointed Ambassador to Kigali a few months later, and got the job without too much difficulty. He declared to whoever would listen that he could have applied for far more illustrious postings, but that he wanted to be close to his fiancée, who, at her father's insistence, really needed to finish her studies at the lycée of Our Lady of the Nile.

The rumor of Frida's engagement caused quite a sensation in Kigali, as well as at the lycée of Our Lady of the Nile, where

Father Herménégilde gave up pursuing Frida with his "rewards," for obvious patriotic reasons. She, however, became insufferably arrogant toward her schoolmates, going so far as to defy Gloriosa, who, powerless, could only swallow her exasperation. But it was at the start of that third year, a few weeks after term began, that Frida unleashed a wave of awe and indignation across the lycée, and not a little envy and admiration.

One Saturday, marked by the successive showers that heralded the rainy season, a procession of four Land Rovers drove through the lycée gates and stopped outside the Bungalow. The driver of the first one rushed to open the rear door, and out climbed a small man dressed in white slacks and a safari jacket, His Excellency Ambassador Balimba. He gave an absentminded greeting to Sister Bursar, who had been placed there to welcome the illustrious visitor. Sister Bursar asked His Excellency to please excuse Mother Superior, who was extremely busy, but that if His Excellency wouldn't mind, she would receive him after High Mass, which His Excellency would surely wish to attend.

While Sister Bursar showed the ambassador around the Bungalow, his liveried servants unloaded huge trunks and swarmed noisily throughout the villa, shifting furniture, piling up groceries and alcohol in the kitchen, unfolding canvas chairs in the living room, placing President Mobutu's portrait on an easel, carting a large bed on a seashell frame edged with gold trim into Monsignor's bedroom, and piling it high with cushions of every shape and color. One of the men rigged up an enormous transistor radio out on the terrace, which immediately began to blast out a deafening throb of rumba live from Kinshasa.

"Frida's not here, my fiancée," said the ambassador. "Quick, go fetch her."

In her panic, Sister Bursar quite forgot to knock, as she burst into Mother Superior's study, where the latter was in conversation with Father Herménégilde and Sister Gertrude.

"Mother! Reverend Mother! If only you knew what . . . if you could hear that music . . . loose women's music . . . at the lycée of Our Lady of the Nile! Mother! If you could see what's happening at the Bungalow! The Congolese ambassador, he's creating havoc, he's moved Monsignor's bed and put a crib of lust in its stead! A den of depravity! And he wants Frida brought to him! Mon Dieu!"

"Calm down, good Sister, calm down. Believe me, I disapprove of this as much as you do, but some things are beyond us, some things we must accept. Let us hope this misdeed will bring a greater good deed . . ."

"Listen, dear Sister," Father Herménégilde interrupted, "as Mother Superior says, it's for the country's good that we must suffer the disorder brought by His Excellency, the Zairian Ambassador. I myself counseled our Mother Superior at the start of the year to accede to His Excellency's requests. Indeed, she received a letter from the Ministry of Foreign Affairs along these lines. You must understand that we have agreed to this for Rwanda, this little country you're so fond of, that you love as much as your homeland, perhaps a little more so. When I was a seminary student, I read a book about the Jews, a secret book written by the Jews themselves, I don't know who brought it to light. The Jews wrote that they wanted to conquer the world, that they had a secret government pulling the strings of every other government, that they had insiders across the board. Well, I'm telling you, the Tutsi are like the Jews. Some missionaries, like old Father Pintard, even say that the Tutsi are really Jews, that it's in the Bible. They may not want to conquer the world, but they do want to seize this whole region. I know they plan a great Hamite empire, and that their leaders meet in secret, like the Jews. Their refugees are everywhere, in Europe, in America. They're hatching every possible plot against our social revolution. Naturally, we've chased them out of Rwanda, and those who've stayed, their accomplices, we're keeping an eye on them, but one day we'll maybe have to get rid of them, too, starting with those who infect our schools and our university. Our poor Rwanda is surrounded by all her enemies: in Burundi, the Tutsi are in power and they're massacring our brothers; in Tanzania, it's the communists; in Uganda, the Bahima, their cousins. Thankfully, we have our great neighbor to support us, our Bantu brother . . ."

"Please, no politics, dear Father, no politics," said Mother

Superior. "Let's simply try to avoid a scandal and keep our innocent girls away."

"But they're engaged, Frida and the ambassador," said Father Herménégilde. "We can say they're here to prepare their marriage, I'm the lycée chaplain . . . Sister Gertrude, go and tell Frida her fiancé is waiting for her. I'll go see them this evening and bring Frida back for refectory."

Shortly before the bell rang for refectory, Father Herménégilde walked up to the Bungalow and addressed the two guards in military fatigues sitting on the front steps.

"Please inform His Excellency that I wish to speak to him and that I have come to escort the young lady back to the lycée."

"The ambassador's not receiving anyone," answered one of the guards in Swahili, "and he said that the girl will stay the night."

"But I am Father Herménégilde, the lycée chaplain, and Frida must come back to the lycée for supper like all the other pupils. I must speak to His Excellency."

"There's no point arguing," said the guard. "It's Monsieur Ambassador who decided the girl would stay the night. You can head back."

"But the young lady can't stay here all night. She's a pupil, we must . . ."

"We'll tell you once again, there's no point arguing," said the other guard, who stood up, revealing his towering frame to Father Herménégilde. "The kid's cool, they don't want to be disturbed."

"But, really . . ."

"I told you there's no point in arguing. The kid's with her fiancé, it's what Monsieur came for."

The giant of a guard slowly came down the steps, and advanced menacingly toward Father Herménégilde.

"All right, all right," said Father Herménégilde, retreating. "Please pay my respects to His Excellency and wish him a good night, I'll see him tomorrow."

Frida remained in the Bungalow with her fiancé until Sunday afternoon. When the convoy of Land Rovers moved off, Frida was seen on the top step of the Bungalow waving expansive good-byes until the cars disappeared around the first bend in the track. A small crowd of pupils in the garden witnessed the scene, held some distance away by Sister Gertrude's threats and a brigade of servants, and when Frida pushed her way through her clustered schoolmates with affected nonchalance, she didn't deign to answer any of the questions they hurled at her.

"Mother, Reverend Mother," said Sister Bursar, as she entered Mother Superior's study, "if you could see the Bungalow! What a mess! And the kitchen . . . And Monsignor's bed . . ."

"Calm down, dear Sister, they won't be coming back. I've negotiated with Monsieur Ambassador, made him see sense, and he's recognized it will be difficult for him to come to the lycée every Saturday and Sunday. He has his diplomatic obligations, and I reminded him that the track gets bad in the rainy season, he might even get stuck. So he agreed, and this is what we decided: whenever it's possible, an embassy car will come and collect Frida on Saturday, then return her on Sunday . . . or maybe on Monday . . . sometimes. Well, they are engaged after all, as Father Herménégilde says . . . and we must render unto Caesar . . ."

For several weeks, an embassy car drove up to fetch Frida each Saturday after midday refectory. The same car deposited her back at school late Sunday night or, more often, on Monday morning. Mother Superior and the monitors pretended not to hear the creaking gate in the middle of the night, and the professors not to notice when Frida suddenly burst into class and noisily took her seat to a murmur of disapproval from her schoolmates. But Frida eventually broke her disdainful silence: she couldn't resist the desire to dazzle her schoolmates with the enthusiastic account of the inimitable life she led with her fiancé. In order to make peace with those girls she'd scorned for so long, and who would remain slyly hostile no matter what she did, Frida brought a whole basket of goodies back from the capital: doughnuts only Swahili mothers know how to make, and above all, the even more exotic brioches and rolls from the Greek baker, as well as sweets from Chez Christina, the shop for whites. There was always some Primus, even a bottle of wine sometimes, preferably Mateus. Practically the whole class managed to squash into Frida's "bedroom," even the class's quota of two Tutsi was invited. When the bell rang for lights-out, the monitor, who had her share of the feast, didn't dare interrupt the fiancée of His Excellency the Ambassador. Frida went over the inventory of her wardrobe at the Zairian Embassy again and again, employing words that didn't fail to impress her audience: evening dress, cocktail dress, culottes, negligé, nightgown. Sometimes she brought one of these prestigious outfits with her, putting it on to elicit wonderment – sincere or feigned – in all the girls. Addressing Immaculée, the acknowledged specialist when it came to beauty products, she listed every skin lightener Ambassador Balimba had recommended to her: makeup remover, foundation, Oriental Blossom lotion, etc. He wanted the whitest fiancée.

"And jewelry?" they asked her anxiously.

Naturally, Monsieur l'Ambassadeur had given jewelry to his fiancée: an engagement ring boasting a huge diamond (in Zaire they walk on diamonds), gold bracelets, vintage ivory bracelets, necklaces of pearls and precious stones. But her fiancé forbade her to wear any outside the embassy. "It would only attract thieves, Kigali's crawling with them! It's too risky: a hand for a basic ring, an arm for a bracelet," he explained. "As for those soldiers and policemen at roadblocks, you never know who you're really dealing with." When Frida wasn't there, the jewelry was strictly locked away in the embassy's enormous safe.

"And your dowry? What's your dad negotiated for your dowry?"

"Don't worry, we're not talking goats or cows here, but money, lots of money! My father and my fiancé are going into business together to set up a transport company. Balimba's putting in all the money, capital he calls it. They'll buy trucks and tanker trucks to carry goods between Mombasa and Kigali, but they'll go further than Kigali, as far as Bujumbura and Bukavu – my fiancé knows the Director of Customs. Ah, if you only you knew what kind of life I'm living with His Excellency Monsieur Ambassador of Zaire my fiancé. We go to all the bars, like the Hôtel des Milles Collines or the Hôtel des Diplomates. And at the French Ambassador's, we eat corned beef that's far tastier than what Sister Bursar gives us for the pilgrimage. And at the Belgian Ambassador's, they serve shellfish from the sea, though I didn't dare try it – it's not fit food for a Rwandan after all . . . And we never drink Primus, but white folks' beer, and when you uncork it – there's no need for a bottle opener – it explodes like thunder and this foam spurts out like smoke from Nyiragongo."

"You think my dad hasn't heard of champagne?" Gloriosa cut in. "He's always got some in his office for visitors, the important ones, he even let me have a taste."

"And me," Godelive said, "you think I haven't seen mussels, I was born in Belgium but I was too young to eat them. My dad often talks about them; says Belgians eat nothing else, and when he goes to Brussels, my mother makes him promise he won't touch them."

Frida was oblivious to the troublemakers:

"If it's a sunny afternoon, we don't take a siesta, we get in the red car, the convertible sports car, and drive out of Kigali, speeding down narrow tracks and causing everyone to flee – women, children, and goats – and men on bicycles to zigzag about and drop their load of bananas and fall into the ditch. We seek out a quiet spot, which isn't easy in Rwanda. One of those places reforested with eucalyptus. Or some rocks up on a ridge. We stop. I press a button. The roof opens. You know, those seats in the little red car are like a bed . . ."

During the heavy rains of November, there was a landslide that carried away all before it – banana trees, houses and their inhabitants – as well as cut off the road that led to the lycée for several weeks. That's when Frida was seized with bouts of nausea, vomiting, and dizziness. She refused to touch the almost daily bulgur in the refectory, and would only eat the corned beef from the French Embassy. The fiancé had been alerted and managed, though nobody knew how, to send her a whole box of it. She wanted her best friends to taste some, but they were wary. Goretti discreetly got hold of one of Frida's empty cans and went to ask Monsieur Legrand, the French teacher with the guitar, what kind of food this might be. Monsieur Legrand explained that it came from a great white bird that was force-fed until it grew ill. Then people ate its illness. All the girls found that disgusting. Only

Immaculée, Gloriosa, Modesta, and Godelive agreed to try some, at Frida's insistence. Their verdict: it was rather soft, and looked like earth, or rather, Goretti said, like the grass that fills a cow's belly and which the Batwa crave after a cow is killed. At any rate, it was real white food, and when it came to white food, they much preferred Kraft cheese and Sister Bursar's deep red corned beef.

It was clear to everyone that Frida was with child, indeed she didn't try to hide it. She was proud to be pregnant, despite the shame it would bring on her family, what with her not being married.

"His Excellency, my fiancé, wants a boy, he's only had girls till now: me, I'll be having a boy."

"So, he's got other women then?" suggested Gloriosa.

"No, he doesn't, not at all," Frida said to reassure herself. "They're either dead or he rejected them."

"And how do you know you'll have a boy?"

"Balimba took every precaution this time. He went to consult a great soothsayer in the forest. It cost him a fortune. The sooth-sayer told him that to cheat the curse his enemies had cast on him, and which made him father only girls, he should wed a girl from the other side of a lake beneath the volcanoes, for the evil spell of the Zairian poisoners would be useless against her. He gave Balimba all the necessary talismans to beget a boy, all the *dawa* whose secrets he knew, for him and for me. I have to wear a belt of pearls and seashells around my belly. It's to have a boy. My fiancé is sure I'll give birth to a boy."

"You should ask Father Herménégilde to bless your belly," said Godelive, "I think he, too, knows every prayer to have babies, or above all, not to have them."

Frida's condition soon worsened, she didn't want to get up, and she complained about agonizing stomach pains. Mother Superior grew anxious and appalled at having to house a pregnant girl in her lycée whose marriage had yet to be celebrated according to the sacraments of the Church. "It's a sin, it's a sin," she repeated to Father Herménégilde, who tried in vain to calm her nagging scruples: "They're engaged, dear Mother, they're engaged; and I'll receive Frida at confession, I will absolve her." Yet Mother Superior couldn't stop her lamentations: "But, Father, have you considered the other innocent pupils? The lycée of Our lady of the Nile will turn into a home for teenage mothers. Oh, the scandal! The scandal!"

Mother Superior sent message after message to the ambassador, begging him to fetch Frida right away, each time exaggerating the urgency and gravity of her state a little more. Balimba finally dispatched a powerful Land Rover, which managed to drive along tracks hitherto considered impassible to any vehicle, and succeeded in reaching the lycée and taking Frida back to Kigali.

News of Frida's death plunged the lycée of Our Lady of the Nile into considerable disarray. Mother Superior decreed a week of mourning to pray for Frida's soul, and at the end of it, on Sunday, the whole school went on a pilgrimage to Our Lady of the Nile so she might shelter that poor little soul beneath her great mantle of mercy. Father Herménégilde decided to give a Mass every morning that week, to the same end. Each class had to attend, one after the other. And the presence of the senior class was of course compulsory at every one. In his funeral oration, Father Herménégilde suggested in passing that the deceased had sacrificed her purity and her youth for the sake of the majority people. Yet neither he nor Mother Superior could hide a certain relief. After all, the drama hadn't occurred within the lycée. Frida's death, as regrettable as it was, put an end to the scandalous example set by tolerating the presence of a pregnant pupil at the school. Allusions to a possible divine punishment having been visited upon the sinful girl were prudently woven into Mother Superior's consoling words to the pupils, and above all in Father Herménégilde's endless moral reflections in religion class.

The seniors remained shut up in their dorm for a whole day – nobody would have dreamed of forcing them to leave it – and, as custom dictated, set to weeping and wailing as one voice. The clamor of their sobbing filled the lycée, the ceaseless tears proof of the sincerity of their sorrow, a remonstration against Frida's undeserved fate. All the girls were united in their despair at being women.

Then the rumors started. What did Frida die of? Why? How? Who had caused her death? The official version made out it was due to complications following a miscarriage. The vehicle driving her back to Kigali must have taken paths that were in poor condition – did the jolts bring it on? In that case, weren't Mother Superior and the ambassador slightly responsible? Why hadn't they waited for the track to be reopened? It was just a matter of days. Or else it was that white food, that part of a sick bird's stomach that Frida gulped down so greedily, that's what poisoned her and her baby. Many thought she'd obviously been poisoned, but not by the white food, by poisoners, Rwandans no doubt. It was easy to understand: Balimba's enemies had her trailed to Kigali, then they paid Rwandan poisoners, *abarozi*; they paid them a fortune, those *abarozi*, an absolute fortune – they're prepared to poison anyone if you give them what they ask, it's their job, they're much more powerful than the Zairian sorcerers and their *dawa*. And also, maybe Frida's ancestors weren't entirely Rwandan, maybe they came from Ijwi Island, or from Bushi, on the other side of the lake . . . So, Balimba . . .

"What I think," said Goretti, "is that her own family killed her, without meaning to of course, by making her abort. That's what would have happened where I'm from. A girl can't get married if she's pregnant or has a baby on her back, even if she's a servant.

It brings dishonor and shame on her and her whole family, she'll draw all kinds of bad luck to them. It's better if the child never existed. So they found a doctor, a bad doctor, it's only bad doctors who perform abortions, or maybe a male nurse, or even worse some doula who made her drink a medicine that causes you to abort or kills you . . . poor Frida! But if what I'm saying is true, Frida's family is right to be scared, for Balimba will take terrible revenge if he's convinced Frida was carrying a boy."

Ambassador Balimba requested his transfer and got it fast. He was posted as part of the Zairian delegation to the Organization of African Unity in Addis Ababa. Frida's father gave up his diplomatic career and threw himself into business. They say he'll do very well at it . . .

"That's enough," Gloriosa said. "I think we've shed enough tears for Frida. We shall mention it no more, either between ourselves or to others. It's time we remembered who we are and where we are. We are at the lycée of Our Lady of the Nile, which trains Rwanda's female elite. We're the ones who've been chosen to spearhead women's advancement. Let us be worthy of the trust placed in us by the majority people."

"Gloriosa," said Immaculée, "do you think it's already time for you to give us one of your politician-type speeches? Like we were at a rally? Women's advancement, well let's talk about that! The reason most of us are here is for our family's advancement, not for our own future but for that of the clan. We were already fine merchandise, since nearly all of us are daughters of rich and powerful people, daughters of parents who know how to trade us for the highest price, and a diploma will inflate our worth even more. I know that a lot of girls here enjoy this game – it's the only game in town, after all – and it's even the source of their pride. But I no longer want to be a part of this marketplace."

"Just listen to her," jeered Gloriosa, "she's talking like a white girl in the movies, or in those books the French teacher makes us read. Where would you be, Immaculée, without your father and his money? Do you think a woman can survive in Rwanda without her family, first her father's then her husband's? You've just come from the gorillas. I suggest you go back there."

"Ah, good advice," said Immaculée. "Perhaps I will."

Once the week of mourning was over, Frida's name was tacitly banned by everyone at the lycée of Our Lady of the Nile. Yet it still tormented the seniors, like one of those shameful words you know without recalling where you got it from nor who taught you it, but which you hear yourself saying without having wanted to. If one of the girls made a slip of the tongue and said the forbidden name, all the other girls turned away, pretended they hadn't heard anything, and began to talk really loudly to cover up, to erase with their pointless chatter, the interminable echo of those two syllables inside their heads. For there was now a shameful secret lying coiled deep within the lycée, and deep within each of the girls, too; remorse in search of a culprit; a sin that could never be purged since it would never be owned. The image must be rejected at all costs: Frida, like that black mirror in which each girl could read her own fate.

The Queen's Umuzimu

Leoncia couldn't wait for Virginia to return home for Easter break. Virginia had always been her mother's favorite child. After all, they had named her Mutamuriza, "Don't Make Her Cry." And now that Virginia was at the lycée – a student! as Leoncia constantly reminded everyone – she was her only pride and joy. Already, she pictured herself accompanying her freshly arrived daughter in her school uniform from enclosure to enclosure greeting everyone who lived on the hill. It would be her glory day! Dressed in her finest wraparound, Leoncia would gauge with either a critical or a satisfied eye just how much respect each neighbor showed her daughter, who would soon return with her diploma, that prestigious Humanities diploma that was awarded so parsimoniously, particularly to girls, and especially Tutsi girls. Even the head of the local Party committee, who always found new ways to harass and humiliate the only Tutsi family on the hill, felt obliged to receive them and to express his congratulations and encouragement, the fulsomeness of which did little to hide the fact he was only doing so out of obligation. Leoncia felt reassured: Virginia was a student, and when you're a student, so she believed, it's as if you're no longer Hutu or Tutsi, but have taken on another "ethnicity": what the Belgians used to refer to as civilized. Virginia would soon be a primary school teacher, maybe even at the nearby mission school, since that's where Father Jerome had first noticed how intelligent she was. He eventually convinced Leoncia that Virginia (her eldest daughter! She to whom her brothers and sisters owed their arrival, their *uburiza*, She who opened their mother's belly for them, She who had to be a little mother for her brothers and sisters) had another future than that of tilling the land alongside them. "A brilliant future," he kept saying, "brilliant!" To persuade Leoncia, he suggested that Virginia could even become a nun with the Benebikira Sisters, not as a cook but as a teacher of course, and later progress to Mother Superior and then Mother General, why not. Leoncia preferred to see her daughter find a good husband, a civil servant obviously, with his own Toyota so he could run a trading business. Already, she was calculating

Virginia's dowry. Not just cows. Also cash to build a brick house, the kind whites live in, with a door and padlocks, and a sheet-metal roof she'd see shining in the sun from far off as she worked her field. And they'd no longer sleep on straw, but on mattresses she'd buy from Gahigi at the market; even the children would have their mattresses, one for the three boys, another for the two girls. And she'd have her own parlor to receive family, friends, and neighbors. Especially the neighbors. They'd sit on folding chairs, not mats. And taking pride of place on the table would be the large shiny golden thermos, always full of tea (three liters!) and always hot, awaiting the arrival of Sunday visitors, who would sip the still-warm tea and chatter to each other as they left. "How lucky Leoncia is to have a daughter who has done advanced studies, she's got a big thermos!"

It rains in March. And in April, it rains even more. Let it rain! Let it rain! The grain lofts will be full and children's tummies bulging. During her two-week vacation, Virginia became the "little mother" again, a position that was hers by right of being the eldest. She looked after her brothers and sisters, and carried her mother's newborn on her back. Leoncia was on vacation too. In the evening, the little ones peppered her with questions, and Virginia regaled them with tales of the wonders of the lycée of Our Lady of the Nile. But it was out in the field that Leoncia truly appreciated her daughter. No, the whites' lycée hadn't changed her. She was the first, before sunrise, to hitch up her wraparound and step barefoot into the mud to wield her hoe. She knew how to track the parasites by making her way between the stems of maize, around which the beanstalks attempted to twine themselves, without crushing the younger shoots sown in December. She could tell the young sorghum from the threatening weeds, which she ripped out, leaping between the mounds of earth covering the sweet potatoes. "Now, that's my daughter!" said Leoncia, "May her name bring her good fortune: Mutamuriza, 'Don't Make Her Cry.'"

It was while pulling up the beans that Virginia told her mother she'd go visit Skolastika, her paternal aunt, the next day.

"Of course you must visit your aunt," said Leoncia. "Why didn't I tell you before? Skolastika's not my sister, she's your father's sister, you're both descended from Nyogosenge. You've got to stay in your aunt's good books, that's what I've always said. Curses upon us should she get in a tiff! A paternal aunt is like a threatening storm. If she were to curse you, what would become of us? Skolastika has always brought you good luck, she'll do the same for your diploma. But you can't visit your aunt empty handed. What would she think of me? Or your father! Take the hoes, we'll go make some sorghum beer for Skolastika."

The whole day was spent making the sorghum beer without which Virginia couldn't visit her aunt. Leoncia was concerned. They were all out of *amamera*, the black sorghum used to make beer, and *umusemburo*, yeast, and had to ask their neighbors. Some didn't have any, others clearly didn't want to give them any. Whatever the outcome, each visit required long exchanges of courtesies. Leoncia tried not to show her impatience. Finally, old Mukanyonga agreed to give them just enough to brew a tiny jugful, following a never-ending monologue about how hard up she was and how tough times were. It doesn't take long to prepare sorghum beer if you've got *amamera* and *umusemburo*, but they had to find a calabash to use as a container, and they needed one with an elegantly curved neck, and gracefully rounded, and they had to pick out one of Leoncia's finely woven baskets to put it in (with a pointy lid), which they decorated with a garland of banana leaves. Then they wrapped the precious gift in a hand towel Virginia had brought back from the lycée, and put it in a little bag.

The pickup stopped at the Gaseke market. Virginia, who, thanks to her school uniform, had managed to sit next to the driver, waited for the enormous woman whose hot, flabby, flesh had squashed her at every bend to extract herself, whining all the while and wiping away the sweat. The passengers at the back had already jumped out and retrieved their luggage: rolled-up mattresses bound with sisal string, sheet metal, a pair of goats, jerricans full of banana beer or petrol. Boys came running from the row of stalls bunched along one side of the muddy market square to unload drums of palm oil and bags of cement that the Pakistani merchant had been impatiently expecting.

Virginia walked into the store, bought a bottle of Primus, then spent a long time haggling at the market with an old grouch over a piece of tobacco, which he cut from a long, plaited spiral. Finally, she made a beeline for the women sitting on their frayed mats selling golden-brown doughnuts from bowls decorated with red flowers. She bought three of them, watched by a row of kids who sat cross-legged opposite the trader, for as long as the market was open, their eyes bright with craving for these inaccessible delights. Virginia walked down the road that led to the hill where her aunt lived.

The narrow path followed the ridge, above the slope of culti-vated terraces that ran down to marshland planted with maize. All the hills, as far as the eye could see, were similarly terraced, and dotted with low houses, some round, some rectangular, their roofs mostly thatched, a few tiled. Many were hidden beneath thick banana groves, their presence betrayed only by the bluish plumes of smoke that stretched out lazily above the large lustrous leaves. Coffee bushes, planted in neat rows, already hung heavy with their bunches of red berries. A few tufts of papyrus sedge man-aged to thrive in the swampy hollows, while four black-crowned cranes strutted with carefree elegance, oblivious to the women working their fields.

On the peak of the highest hill stood the impressive buildings of the mission. The church's crenellated tower reminded Virginia of a picture in her history book: the fortress in Europe where noble knights once lived, according to Sister Lydwine's oft-repeated lesson.

The sun was about to dip beyond the hills when Virginia glimpsed her auntie's house at the end of the path. Skolastika, who must have recognized her niece's silhouette from far off, immediately left her field, gathered in her basket the sweet potatoes she'd just unearthed for the evening meal, raced uphill, and prepared to welcome her guest at the entrance to the enclosure before Virginia could get there. Skolastika barely had time to rip up a handful of grass with which to brush the dried earth from her legs and feet, before smoothing down the wraparound she'd hoisted above her calves to work the field. Virginia had removed the basket from the bag and balanced it on her head, as custom demands. "Welcome, Virginia," said Skolastika. "I knew you were coming, I was informed of it. Last night, the fire began to crackle, sparks dancing above the flames. It was a sign I would receive a visit. So then I spoke the words one must utter at such a moment. '*Arakaza yizaniye impamba*, may my guest not arrive empty handed!' But I knew very well it was you who was coming. I am Nyogosenge, your paternal aunt. Leoncia had to let you come."

She bade Virginia enter the yard and the pair of them walked up to the house. Skolastika stood at the threshold, and Virginia gracefully bent forward so her aunt could take the basket with both hands, then go and put it down, slowly and carefully, on the shelf behind the door, before it took its place of honor between the churns and the milk pails.

Now it was time for the welcome greetings. Skolastika and Virginia shared a long and close embrace, patting each other while the aunt whispered the long litany of wishes in her niece's ear: "*Girumugabo*, may you find a husband! *Girabana benshi*, and bear many children! *Girinka*, may you have cows aplenty! *Gira amashyo*, a plentiful herd! *Ramba, ramba*, long life! *Gira amahoro*, may peace be with you! *Kaze neza*, you are welcome here!"

Skolastika and Virginia entered the house together, and Skolastika opened Virginia's basket, took out the calabash, selected two straws from their quiver-shaped case and handed them both to Virginia. The two women squatted down opposite each other, and Skolastika placed the gourd between them. They each sucked up a mouthful of beer, and Skolastika gave a deep and appreciative sigh that expressed her contentment.

The first day of Virginia's stay at her aunt's was, of course, a series of triumphal visits to the neighbors. That night, Skolastika recounted to all the assembled family every single mark of respect her lycée niece had received, even from Rugaju, the pagan, indeed Skolastika made the most of Rugaju's words to suggest he get his children christened – at least the boys – so they could attend school like everyone else. Skolastika's husband questioned Virginia at length about her studies: he'd spent two years at the local seminary and proudly showed her the three books on arithmetic, grammar, and conjugations he kept safely stored away as testimony to his advanced studies. Skolastika didn't seem to appreciate her husband's interest in her niece. At bedtime, after much beating around the bush and exaggerated expressions of deference, apology, and respect, Virginia finally told her aunt that she wouldn't be going to the mission the next day as planned. She had to go see Clotilde, her childhood friend, with whom she'd played, danced, and skipped rope with whenever she visited Skolastika. She'd heard that Clotilde had gotten married and just had a child. She'd promised to visit her as soon as she arrived. Skolastika was somewhat shocked at the bold manner in which Virginia addressed her paternal aunt, but she chose not to show her irritation. Virginia was a student, after all, her teachers at the lycée were white, and there were some things you just couldn't understand about people who always lived among whites. "Very well," said Skolastika, "go and see Clotilde, and you'll come with me to the mission the day after tomorrow. Father Fulgence wants to see you."

Virginia was a little anxious when she said good-bye to her aunt before leaving to go see Clotilde. But Skolastika let none of her disappointment show, and even gave her a handful of *igisukari* bananas – the sweetest of sweet things – for Clotilde and her baby. Virginia put the bananas in her bag and set off to her friend's house. However, just after she'd passed the little grove of reforested eucalyptus, she switched direction and, after several long detours, reached a steep path leading down to the swamp. Halfway down it was Rugaju the pagan's house. Scruffy kids were playing in the yard, running about and squabbling. As soon as they saw Virginia enter the yard, they froze in astonishment.

Virginia motioned to the tallest kid, who looked about ten.

"Come here, I've got something to tell you."

The boy hesitated, then shoved his brothers and sisters out of the way and walked over to Virginia.

"What's your name?"

"Kabwa."

"Hey, Kabwa, do you know Rubanga? Do you know where he lives?"

"Rubanga, the witch doctor? Sure, I know Rubanga. I've been to his place a few times with my dad. No one but my dad goes to see that old jabberer. Folks say he's crazy, they also say he's a poisoner."

"I want you to take me to Rubanga."

"You, the student, take you to Rubanga! You must have someone to poison!"

"There's no one I want to poison. I want to ask him something. To do with the lycée."

"The lycée? They do some strange stuff at the white school!"

"I'll give you some doughnuts if you take me."

"Doughnuts?"

"And a Fanta."

"An orange Fanta?"

"An orange Fanta and doughnuts."

"If you really give me an orange Fanta, I'll take you to Rubanga's place."

"The orange Fanta and the doughnuts are in my bag. As soon as I see Rubanga's place, they're yours. But then you leave and you don't say anything to anyone. Did they ever tell you the story about the evil stepmother and the kid who's not hers that she put to sleep in the mortar? I'll ask Rubanga to cast a spell on you; if you tell, you'll end up like that kid in the mortar: you'll stop growing and you'll never get a beard."

"I won't say anything, not even to my father, but show me the orange Fanta, I want to make sure you're not lying."

Virginia opened her bag and showed him the Fanta and the doughnuts.

"Follow me," said Kabwa.

Virginia and her guide got back on the path that ran steeply down to the swamp. She covered her head with her wraparound, for fear of being recognized, but few women ventured into the valley during the rainy months, and what's more, the narrow path petered out at the end of the swamp, an area that was enclosed by the steep hills and that hadn't been cultivated yet.

Kabwa pointed at a gap in the thick papyrus sedge.

"Careful you don't stray either left or right," Kabwa said. "You'll get stuck in the mud, and don't count on me to drag you out, I'm not strong enough. And if you spot the hippopotamus, just give way, it's his trail but don't be scared." Kabwa chuckled. "He only comes out of his pool at night."

They pushed on beneath the canopy of diaphanous papyrus plumes. Virginia tried not to pay any mind to the continual gurgling that rose from the murky water of the swamp, or to the slimy convulsions of the black mud.

"We're here," said Kabwa.

The papyrus sedge thinned out, revealing a rocky islet, as if its thorny bushes had decided to wander off into the middle of the swamp.

"Look," said Kabwa, pointing to a hut atop the little rise, "that's Rubanga's place. Now I've brought you where you wanted to go, give me what you promised me."

Virginia handed him the Fanta and the doughnuts, then Kabwa sped off and disappeared through the breach in the papyrus sedge.

When Virginia drew near the hut, she saw a little old man reclining on a tattered mat. He was wrapped in a brownish blanket and wore a woolly hat with a fat red pom-pom. A wooden peg clipped his nostrils together.

Virginia advanced slowly, giving little coughs to signal her arrival. The old man didn't seem to register her presence.

"Rubanga," she said softly, "Rubanga, I've come to say hello."

Rubanga raised his head and took a long look at her.

"You've come to say hello, a beautiful young lady like you! Now, let me look at you, it's been so long since such a beautiful young lady as yourself came to see me. Sit down in front of me, so the sun shines on your face."

Virginia squatted down on her heels.

"There, now I can see your face. Do you want some tobacco, like me? I've stuffed my nose full of it, see. In the old days, great ladies liked to stuff their noses with tobacco."

"No, Rubanga, these days, young women don't take snuff. Here, I've brought you this," she said, handing him the bottle of Primus and the piece of plaited tobacco wrapped in banana bark.

"You came all this way, to the farthest reaches of the marsh, to bring me a bottle of Primus! You're not my daughter. What's your name? What do you want from me?"

"My name is Virginia, my real name is Mutamuriza. I'm at the lycée. I know that you know a lot about the olden times. That's what everyone in Gaseke says. I've come to hear about the queens from long ago. What happened to them when they died? I know that you know about that."

"One must never say that the Queen is dead. Never. Don't ever say that again, it could bring you misfortune. And you want to know what happened to them?"

"Tell me. I need to know."

Rubanga turned away, unclipped his nose peg, and pressing

each nostril with his index finger, snorted out a brownish stream. He wiped his teary eyes with the back of his hand, cleared his throat, spat forcefully, folded his legs, and took his head in his emaciated hands. His thin, quavering voice grew stronger as he spoke.

"Don't ask me. It's a secret. An *ibanga*. A secret of the kings. And I am one of the guardians of the kings' secrets. I am an *umwiru*. You know my name, my name carries the secret. I don't know all the kings' secrets. I only know those given me to safeguard. The *abiru* don't give away their secrets. In my family, we never revealed the secrets entrusted to our memory by the King. I know of some who sold their secrets to the whites. The whites wrote the secrets down. They even made a book out of them, so I gather. But what do the whites understand of our secrets? It will bring them misfortune. There's even a Rwandan *umupadri* who tried to pass himself off as an *umwiru*. He also wrote the secrets down. It brought us misfortune. In olden days, the King would have had him killed. His *batwa* would have poked out his eyes and ripped out his tongue before throwing him into the Nyabarongo. Well, me, I've kept the secret the King entrusted me with. Now folks make fun of me. The *abapadri* say I'm a sorcerer. The mayor's thrown me in prison more than once. I don't know why. They say I'm crazy. But my memory hasn't forgotten a word of what the King entrusted to my family. For an *umwiru*, forgetting means death. The King sometimes summoned all the *abiru* to court. He gave them cows, and jugs of mead. All the court grandees honored them. But the great *abiru*, those who know every single secret – there were four of them, the eldest was Munanira – tested their memory. It was like the national exam people go on about today. Misfortune would fall upon he who forgot anything. All it took was the slightest hesitation, the slightest omission, and he would be dismissed, sent home for the shame he'd brought on himself and his kin.

"There are no kings left now, the great *abiru* are dead, they were either killed or went into exile. So I tell my secrets to the red blooms of the flame tree. I check carefully that no one can hear me apart from the red flowers of the tree, the blood of Ryangombe, the Master of Spirits. But children often follow me, they hide and listen to what I am reciting, and when I discover them and chase them away, they scatter, crying out: '*Umusazi! Umusazi!* He's crazy! he's crazy!' And if they tell their mother what they've heard and seen, she'll say: 'You're not to breathe a word of what you've seen, don't tell a soul what you've heard, nobody, neither your neighbor, nor your teacher, nor the *umupadri*. Don't speak of it. Forget what you've heard and seen. Never mention it.' Now tell me, why did you come to see me? Want me to reveal my secrets to you, too? Do you want to sell them to the Bazungu? Or put them in a book? A lovely young lady like yourself, do you want to draw misfortune upon you?"

"I won't reveal your secrets. If you tell me, I'll keep them to myself, locked in my memory, I won't share them with anyone. The reason I've come is, well, I think I've been sent to you by a Queen, a Queen from long ago."

"A Queen from long ago? You've seen her *umuzimu*?"

"Maybe. Let me tell you. I went to a white man's place with my friend. He's really crazy. He believes we Tutsi are Egyptians and that we came from Egypt. You know all that stuff the whites invented about the Tutsi. He discovered a Queen's tomb on his estate. He dug up her bones, but didn't hand them over to the museum. He erected a monument on top of them. He explained to us that's what the black queens called Candace did. He wanted me to be Queen Candace for him. He showed us some photos. I've no idea what you're supposed to do with a queen's bones. I've heard tell that a python watched over her in those olden days. I didn't see any python, but I did see the Queen. I saw her in my dreams. Not very clearly. Like a cloud. A strip of cloud that frays as it catches the mountain slope, sun sparkling through it from time to time. A shining cloud, but I know it's the Queen. Sometimes, through that mask of droplets of light, I make out her face. I think she's asking me to do something for her. She won't leave me be. You, who know the secrets of the kings, tell me what I must do."

"Where do you come from?"

"I'm staying with my paternal aunt, Mukandori."

"I know your aunt. I know your family. You have a good lineage. It's mine, also. So that's why I'll tell you what I can tell you. But don't say anything to anyone, do you hear me? Make sure your aunt, who wears a rosary hung around her neck and is always up at the mission, doesn't know you've been here. Don't tell those whites who want to know everything but who understand nothing. I want to help you and the *umuzimu*, especially the Queen's *umuzimu*. I think the white man woke the *umuzimu* from its deep sleep. And when you wake Spirits from the peaceful slumber of their death, they're furious. They can change into a leopard, or a lion, that's what folk believed in the olden times.

"I went to a Queen's funeral once, a very long time ago. We weren't supposed to say the Queen was dead. We said: 'She's drunk the mead.' I was young. I went with my father. 'Come along,' he said. 'Everything you see me do today will fall upon you to do one day. Then I'll pass the secret on to you, the secret the King entrusted to our family for safekeeping. You too will pass it on to one of your sons.' My father was wrong: I never followed in his footsteps. My sons attended the whites' school. They're ashamed of their father. The secret will disappear with me. Now you, you're young, you've come all this way, so I'll tell you how a Queen was accompanied to her final resting place, listen carefully, and I think you'll find what you're after.

"To start with, the Queen's body was left to dry. The *abiru* lit a fire beneath her deathbed. They turned her over so she'd dry out all through. They'd wrapped her in cloth made from fig tree. Now my father was a great *umwiru*. He'd brought a cow for the Queen.

He'd given me a large milk pot to carry, an *igicuba*, which had been carved especially and had never had any milk in it. My father milked the cow to give milk to the Queen. Here's where you've got to pay attention. There was a woman with us. A young virgin. She wasn't an *umwiru*. There are no women *umwiru*. She was one of the queen's Retainers. She was chosen because she was the Queen's favorite retainer, her *inkundwakazi*. I gave her the big pot full of milk. She went to take it to the Queen. It was for the Queen's *umuzimu*. Did you listen properly? She was a young virgin, the Queen's favorite retainer, the one chosen to take her the milk. Then we went to the place the spells had designated as the Queen's resting place. The journey took four days. Every evening, we were welcomed at a lodge built especially to host the Queen and all the *abiru*. There were aplenty of jugs of beer, sorghum, bananas, and mead waiting for us. Once we left, the inn was destroyed. At the Queen's resting place, we built a hut and an enclosure. A hut for the Queen, a hut for us, the *abiru*. My father's only task was to milk the cow, mine to hand the milk pot to the retainer, and the retainer's to carry it to the Queen's bed. We spent four months with her. We received beer and provisions in abundance. Four months later, an envoy arrived from the king to announce the end of mourning. We departed. We left the Queen's dwelling standing, so it would collapse of its own accord. The fig trees in the enclosure would grow into tall trees. They would soon become like a small forest: the Queen's *kigabiro*. No one must set foot inside! And there was also a tall tree, a flame tree, though it hadn't been planted by us. It was already very high. I think it was because of that tree that the *abiru* had decided to lay the Queen in that place. The flame tree is covered in flowers during the dry season: it's the only tree among them all that agreed to receive Ryangombe after the buffalo gored him, those red flowers are his blood. The Queen's spirit did not linger in the tomb, by her bones, those red blossoms received the queen's *umuzimu*. Curses upon anyone who takes his ax to that tree!

"I can't tell you what happened to the Queen's retainer. I don't know. Perhaps she remained with the Queen, close by. Don't ask me.

"That's what I saw, that's what I know, that's what I can tell you. It's because I believe you really saw the spirit of the Queen that I've revealed all this to you. That white man awoke her *umuzimu*. It needs calming, it needs to sink back into the slumber of death. If the Queen is pursuing you in your dreams, it could be that she's seeking her retainer, the one who was her favorite, who was always at her side, who supported her, for the queens found it hard to walk because of the weight of the metal anklets that were piled knee-high. She's looking for the girl who gave her the milk, even after her death, when the slumber of death hadn't yet dulled her mind. The Queen's shadow must dissolve in the mist of Death, and she must disappear again; otherwise, she'll continue to torment you, and torment the living, she'll torment you until you join her in the land of the dead. Come back and see me, and I'll tell you what you must do."

"I will come back, but promise me you'll keep this Queen at bay or else make her look upon me favorably."

"I will tell you what you should do and I'll give you what you'll need to do that: I'm an *umwiru*."

"You're back late," said Clotilde. "I'd given up waiting. I didn't think you were coming."

"You know what it's like with paternal aunts, the respect you must show them, they like to make the most of it. She gave me permission to come and see you, but just as I was heading off, she found all these excuses to detain me as long as possible, a way of reminding me of her authority. What can you do in the face of your paternal aunt's goodwill?"

Two days before her departure, Virginia got permission from Skolastika to go say good-bye to Clotilde. "I didn't realize you were so fond of that Clotilde," said her aunt with an air of bitterness and suspicion, "though far be it from me to contradict such an educated girl. You know what you're doing. Go and bid farewell to your dear friend before you leave."

Just after the eucalyptus grove, Virginia took the path down to the swamp.

"You're going to see the witch doctor again," said Kabwa as she passed Rugaju's house. "Shall I show you the way?"

"I no longer have need of you, now that I know the way. Even though Kabwa's your name, I don't need a little dog trailing me."

"Give me something, all the same."

"You know what I asked Rubanga regarding you: if you tell, misfortune will befall you. But, here, take this coin anyway."

"I didn't see you, and I won't say a thing, I promise."

Virginia pushed farther into the papyrus sedge, jumping at the rustlings, twitchings, flutterings, and scramblings that filled the swamp with a myriad of living things always close by but never seen. At last, she emerged at the foot of Rubanga's hillock.

Just like on her first visit, she found him squatting by his hut, but without his snuff clip.

"I've been waiting for you," said Rubanga. "I knew the day you were going to come. We *abiru* have something of the soothsayers, the *abafumu*. You did well to come back, not just for your sake, but above all for the Queen's *umuzimu*. She's suffering, poor Queen. In discovering her bones, that white man woke her from the slumber of death, and she sought refuge in your dreams, she wanders them, she chose you to be her retainer, her favorite. She's counting on you to take her back to the land of the dead, for you to be her companion there, but you're far too young to go to the land of the dead. So I went on your behalf, to that place where no one must venture. What I'm about to tell you is the great secret, or at least part of the great secret. If I tell you, you'll become an *umwiru*, not entirely, because there are no women *abiru*, but you'll share a little of the secret. So I've prepared some of what the *abiru* must drink to preserve the secret."

He handed her a small calabash and a straw.

"You're to drink this."

"Why do you want me to drink that? What is it?"

"Don't worry, it's not poison, well, not yet. It's *igihango*, and you must drink it. All *abiru* must drink it. Drink, it will protect you, but if you betray the secret, the *igihango* will turn into poison. Sickness and misfortune will befall you and your entire family. If you break the secret, the secret will break you."

"I trust you, I've got no choice. Give me your calabash. I won't break the secret."

Virginia gulped, and a sour fiery liquid filled her mouth. She squeezed back her tears.

"Good, that's very brave of you. Now, listen to me. I went to the swamp, the great endless swamp of Nyabarongo, on your behalf and for the Queen's *umuzimu*. There's no path; if you step into it and sink, you'll be walking forever and never get out. But I know how to reach this little hut, not just any hut, even though it looks like a hunter's shelter, it's the House of the Drum. You can't see the Drum when you enter the hut, for it's buried, deep down in the earth beneath you. It's Karinga, the Drum of the kings, the Drum of Rwanda, the Root of Rwanda: it holds all of Rwanda in its entrails. Have you ever heard Karinga roar? Now, when Karinga rumbled – for Karinga wasn't beaten like any other drum, Karinga rumbled of its own accord – the whole of Rwanda heard it, they said that everything under the sun heard it, women suddenly stood still, leaning on their hoes, men's hands froze above their beer jug, unable to plunge the straw in, the hunter pulling back the string of his bow couldn't release his arrow, the shepherd playing his flute lost his breath, cows forgot to graze, and mothers to breastfeed their babies. When Karinga ceased rumbling, it was as if the country awoke from some great bewitchment. No one could say for how long Karinga had thundered. Karinga's enemies pursued him and sought to burn him, so Karinga buried himself in the earth. His enemies looked for him but never found him. Perhaps Karinga will surge forth from the earth one day. Nobody knows when. But buried in the ground, he still watches over Rwanda, for no one has been able to expose the contents of the drum's belly. Even I don't know. Nobody has seen Karinga's heart. It's the secret of secrets."

Rubanga's voice trembled as he uttered the drum's name. He stayed silent for a while.

"Well . . . now . . . listen carefully to what I've done for you and the Queen's *umuzimu* . . . I lay down just above the spot where the Drum is buried, and in my dream, the Drum revealed to me what I must do for the Queen's *umuzimu*. What you must do for the Queen's *umuzimu*. You've attended the whites' school, but you're still a virgin. So I've carved this small milk pot for you out of flame-tree wood, a little milk pot, like for a child. The dead aren't greedy, a few drops will satisfy them. And I'm giving you this leafy branch. It's *umurembe*, a plant that soothes the dead because it has no thorns. Long ago, before the missionaries came, these leaves would be placed in the deceased's hand. You're to return to that white man with this pot and these leaves. You must fill the little pot with milk, milk from an *inyambo* cow, do you hear, not milk from any other cow. And the milker must be an *intore*, a strong young warrior. You're to go up to the *kigabiro* surrounding the tomb. One of the trees is a flame tree, I saw it in my dream. You're to dip the leaves in the milk and sprinkle the flame tree, saying: 'Return without thorns, like the *umurembe*.' When the pot's empty, bury it at the foot of the tree. But take great care that the pot doesn't touch the ground before that; otherwise, it will lose its power. Remember all I've said and tell no one."

"You still playing goddess at that crazy Whitey's place?" asked Virginia.

"Why not?" replied Veronica. "He dresses me up as an Egyptian, covers me with perfume and incense, photographs me, draws me, paints me. But he doesn't touch me: I'm his statue, his doll, his goddess. I dance before She whom he painted in my likeness and sometimes I feel as if I, too, have been transported to another world."

"I think you've been seized by old Fontenaille's madness. You scare me. I don't know where this is all going to lead you."

"What's there to lose? You and me, I often wonder what's the point of us continuing to study in this high school where they train, as they say, the so-called female elite. We'll never be a part of their elite. We get the best grades, not because we're the most intelligent but because we just have to be the best, and we make believe our good grades will protect us, that thanks to them, we may still be a little hopeful about our future. But look at the others: for some of them at least, coming to class is purely a formality, it's like they'd already got the diploma, it's like they were already some minister's wife, they go along to class like a bureaucrat goes along to his office, grades are secondary, that's not what interests them. But you and me, what's to become of us? A Tutsi diploma isn't the same as a Hutu diploma. It's not a real diploma. That diploma is your meal ticket. If it's marked Tutsi on it, you'll never find a job, not even working for the whites. That's the quota for you."

"I know all that, and I often tell myself I should have stayed and farmed on my hill. But my mother imagines the diploma will save everything, me and my family . . . So, you're still going to see your Whitey."

"Yes, of course, he sent those portraits he made of me off to Europe, says they went down very well, and the photos too, that he made some money off them, he says that I truly am his goddess, that I bring him good luck, that this money is for me, too, and that part of it will pay for my studies in Europe. And he even says that now I'm known in Europe, they're expecting me. I might become a star, like in the movies. Fontenaille may be a crazy fool, but he's a crazy fool who made his delusions a reality, and maybe he'll make my dreams come true. Him, he lives in his dream. He's hired young men who didn't pass their national exam or who were kicked out of the core curriculum because of the quota. He wants them to live like the Tutsi of olden days. He's even taken on a former courtier to teach them to dance. They're his shepherds, his dancers, his *intore*, his Egyptian warriors. The boys accept it, he pays them well and makes these vague promises about finding them a school later on, I don't know how. Meanwhile, he lectures them at length about their Egyptian roots. I'm afraid some will end up believing him. He no longer knows who he is, sometimes he's a great Tutsi chief, sometimes a priest of Isis. He also told me some journalists would be coming from Europe to do a report about him and his temple. They're even going to make a little movie. I'm going to act in their movie. I'll be the goddess, the star. If only they could take me away with them!"

"You're dreaming too. Fontenaille's madness will get the better of you. Watch out for that. But I'd like to go to Fontenaille's place on Sunday."

"See, you too want to act out the white's crazy notions. Come along, he can't wait to see you. He's always asking me where his Queen Candace is, if she'll be coming back one day. He'll be mad with joy to see you return and to dress you as Queen Candace. He showed me the outfit that awaits you, and you alone."

"It's not to dress up as Queen Candace that I want to go there, it's for something that I can't tell you about. I have to go on my own. Please, don't be cross, I don't want to take your place, I don't want to play Queen Candace every Sunday, but I need to go there once by myself."

"I don't understand it at all, but you're my friend, so I trust you. I don't think you're out to trick me. Whatever it is must be really important for you to go to Fontenaille's, but it's quite mysterious of you! Sunday, you'll go to Rutare, to those massive rocks, where the jeep will be waiting. I'll give you a letter for Fontenaille saying that I'm sick and that I'm sending you instead. He'll be pleased to have his Candace, but still, I don't understand it at all . . ."

"I can't tell you anything, it would bring us both misfortune."

"It's my Candace!" cried Monsieur de Fontenaille, seeing Virginia climb out of the jeep clutching her bag to her chest. "I was expecting her, I knew she would come back to me one day. But where is Isis?"

"Veronica is unwell. She's written you a letter."

Monsieur de Fontenaille read the letter. Dismay spread across his face.

"Don't worry," Virginia reassured him. "Veronica will always be your Isis, she'll be here next Sunday, and today I will happily be your Queen Candace, but on one condition."

"On one condition?"

"There's a real Queen on your estate. You've built a pyramid over her remains. I'm scared she won't put up with seeing another queen here. As you know, we Rwandans are quite fearful of the spirits of the dead: they can turn evil if we offend them. I'm not really a queen, and if Nyiramavugo sees me dressed up as a queen, her spirit will become enraged, she'll pursue me – and you, too – seeking revenge. So, first I need to make her an offering to reconcile us."

Monsieur de Fontenaille hesitated for a moment, trying to understand what Virginia meant, what lay behind her words. Then, he seemed overcome with sudden elation.

"Yes, yes, my queen . . . of course, you must pay homage to the former Queen, to she who lies beneath the pyramid of the Candace queens. And you, whom I saw on the stele at Meroë, you will make whole the chain of time again."

Monsieur de Fontenaille closed his eyes as if dazzled by the unbearable brilliance of a vision, his hands were shaking. After a long moment that Virginia thought would never end, he became calm again.

"What do you want to do, my Queen? I'll do everything you tell me to do."

"It's just a matter of giving the Queen that which a Rwandan holds most dear: milk. And you have the right milk for a queen: that which comes from *inyambo* cows."

Virginia took out the little pot from her bag, as well as the leafy *umurembe* branch.

"We need to fill up my little milk pot, it's just the right amount to soothe the queen."

"Follow me. My shepherds will fill your pot with this morning's milking, then we'll climb up to the Queen's tomb so you can carry out your duties to her."

"Monsieur de Fontenaille," said Virginia as he made to enter the funereal grove with her, "please don't be angry with me, but I must proceed alone into the *kigabiro*. It's a forbidden wood. You must have cut down trees, you dug up the earth, uncovered the Queen's remains, and built your monument on top. You're a white man, but you've violated the *kigabiro* all the same. I'm afraid that the Queen will refuse my offering if you're with me. If we annoy the dead, we may have to fear their evil. Perhaps this is of no concern to you whites, but it's me who'll receive her vengeance. Please, don't be angry, I beg you."

"But of course I'm not angry, Candace. On the contrary, I understand, I respect the rituals. When you get back to the villa, you'll dress yourself in Queen Candace's clothes again. I'll do your portrait. Isis, Candace, the evidence is accumulating. Even if the Tutsi were to disappear, I am the custodian of their legend."

Virginia slipped between the gnarled trunks of the ancient fig trees, avoiding the clearing where the pyramid stood, trying to find the flame tree in the eerie and closely growing thicket. A thought entered her head: "What if the python is stalking me from within the undergrowth?" She hurried and soon reached the far side of the wood: "Rubanga deceived me," she said to herself. "He's just an old charlatan." But as soon as she got out into the open, she saw a tree standing on its own not far away. It wasn't covered with red blossoms (she knew it only flowered in the dry season), but she recognized it as the tree she sought from its twisting branches and cracked bark: the flame tree, the *umurinzi*, the guardian, as it should be called out of respect, the tree the *abiru* chose long ago to receive the Queen's *umuzimu*. She circled it, plunged the *umurembe* stem into the pot, and sprinkled the *umurinzi* with milk drops while reciting the words: "Return without thorns, like the *umurembe*." When the little pot was empty, she knelt at the foot of the tree and dug a hole with a flat stone, in which she buried the pot and the *umurembe* branch. When she stood up, she thought she saw the flame tree's leaves tremble and she felt as if bathed with a serene strength. "From now on," she thought, "the Queen's *umuzimu* will bring me good fortune, I am her favorite, but her favorite in this world."

As they walked back down to the villa, the servant ran toward them and breathlessly announced:

"Master! Master! There's a visitor: the old padre, the one with a big beard. He came on his *ipikipiki*."

"That old Father Pintard, he still rides that motorbike at his age! He's back again to convert me to his biblical absurdities. He'll try to convert you, too. Twenty years, he's been trying. Don't listen to him. And don't forget it was me who told you where you come from, from Meroë, I recognized you as Queen Candace."

Father Pintard was waiting in the large living room. The little bamboo chair he was sitting on seemed ready to collapse beneath his imposing stature. His white cassock spattered with mud was swathed in chunky rosary beads, like a hunter with his cartridge belts. His long patriarch's beard made a big impression on Virginia.

"Fontenaille, hello, I see you're still attracting gullible young ladies to your demonic chapel. If it's for your perversions, which reassures me a little, then it must be because you're so well past it that your true favorites are queens from four thousand years ago."

"Bless me, Father, for I have greatly sinned," replied Fontenaille, laughing. "This young lady's name is Virginia, I'm drawing her portrait and you'll see how much she resembles a queen from two thousand years ago."

"Dear girl, don't listen to Fontenaille, listen to me instead, you're Tutsi I presume, in any case there are only ever Tutsi at Fontenaille's. When I arrived in Rwanda, almost forty years ago now, people swore by Tutsi and only Tutsi, bishops as much as Belgians. They'd had to change kings, but we were soon to baptize the new one, it was Constantin they wanted. Then the Belgians and bishops turned coats: they swore by Hutu and Hutu only, the doughty democratic farmers, the Lord's humble sheep. Well, I've got no views on the matter, I obey Monsignor, and those young missionaries just fall for everything they're told about the majority *demokarasi*. But I've spent nearly forty years studying: the Bible on the one hand, the Tutsi on the other. It's all in the Bible, the story of the Tutsi and everything else."

"Pintard! Pintard! That's nonsense! Don't exhaust us with your ridiculous theories. Virginia doesn't want to hear it."

But Father Pintard didn't want to hear it either. He had launched himself, apparently still addressing Virginia, into an endless monologue, part sermon, part lecture. "Without going as far back as Noah, let's start with Moses. The Israelites left Egypt, Moses parted the waters of the Red Sea with his staff, but some of them went the wrong way, heading south, and arrived in the land of Kush, these were the first Tutsi, then there was the Queen of Sheba, who was also Tutsi, and she went to visit Solomon and returned home with the child she begat with the great king, and then her son became emperor of a land where the Jews were Tutsi called Falashas," and at the end of all that, Virginia hadn't understood why it should finish in Rwanda, where the Tutsi were the real Jews, along with the *abiru* who knew the secrets of King Solomon's mines.

Monsieur de Fontenaille laughed, threw his hands in the air, poured glass after glass of whiskey, and offered some to his guest, who refused more and more feebly until he eventually accepted. Virginia didn't dare interrupt Father Pintard, but when she noticed the sun was close to setting, she whispered in Fontenaille's ear:

"It's late, I must get back to the lycée, I need a lift."

"Please excuse me, Father," Fontenaille interrupted. "Virginia must get back to the lycée. I'll tell my driver to take her back. Now, Virginia, promise me you'll return on Sunday: I want to see you as Queen Candace."

"Young lady," said Father Pintard, "think hard about what I've told you. You'll find some consolation in my words for your people's misfortune."

"Tell me, Virginia, did you play the queen at Fontenaille's?" asked Veronica.

"I did what I needed to do. But I also learned that Tutsi aren't humans: here, we're *inyenzi*, cockroaches, snakes, rodents; to whites, we're the heroes of their legends."

King Baudouin's Daughter

After the Easter break, Mother Superior wanted to show just how far her liberalism extended: she gave the girls permission to decorate the partitions of their "rooms." With taste and moderation, she had insisted, and distributed drawings of Our Lady of the Nile that they could hang over their beds. Gloriosa checked to make sure that all the girls had placed the President's photo next to Our Lady of the Nile. In Rwanda, all human activity took place beneath the curatorial portrait of the President. In even the most humble boutiques, the head of state's dusty red portrait stood guard atop a shelf, flanked by a few bags of salt, some matches, and three cans of Nido milk; in even the sleaziest of bars, the portrait swung above jugs of banana beer and a lone crate of Primus bottles. The living rooms of the rich and powerful competed to have the largest, since the size of the President's portrait testified to the businessman's or civil servant's unswerving loyalty to the Emancipator of the majority people. Unfortunate is the lady of the house who neglects to divest the beloved leader's portrait of the tiniest speck of dust each morning.

Goretti was the only one who dared criticize the venerated photo: "I like our President very much," she remarked, "but at least he could've dressed like a president for the photo, with a peaked cap, a smart uniform with epaulettes, loads of braid on the sleeves, and a heap of medals on his jacket. That's what every president looks like, but ours looks like a seminary student in that dinky suit." The girls around her pretended not to have heard. They awaited Gloriosa's reaction. She took her time to retort, and surprised everyone with her moderation: "Our President doesn't need a uniform to address the people, they all understand him, not like you and your colonel father." Making fun of the way people spoke in the North, where they lived alongside gorillas at the foot of the volcanoes, was just part of the joking around that hardly shocked anyone. So nobody understood why Gloriosa hadn't deployed her usual arsenal of threats, like denouncing remarks of her being subversive with regard to the Party and, even worse, her father . . . The most perceptive deduced that the military, particularly officers who came from the North, were clearly becoming quite influential, and that the President himself had to reckon with them. Goretti's behavior suddenly seemed less awkward, and her language less rude. The girls refrained from the customary teasing and showered Goretti with signs of affection and solicitation, which she received with disdainful benevolence.

It proved to be quite difficult for the girls to decorate their alcove partitions as recommended by Mother Superior. They hung up some small basketwork panels decorated with traditional geometric motifs, place mats embroidered with simplistic flowers, photos of parents or entire families taken at an elder sister or brother's wedding. But the girls weren't satisfied with the result: this wasn't how a young, modern girl, a "civilized" girl as they would say during the Colonial Era, should decorate her room. What was needed, and they knew it, were pictures of young people with long hair, singers wearing "anti-sun" shades, as they were called, blond girls, real blondes, blonder than Madame de Decker, long-blond-haired beach girls in bathing suits like the ones in the movies at the French Cultural Center. Of course there were no such pictures at the lycée of Our Lady of the Nile, except perhaps, said Immaculée, among the French teachers, who were young and single, most likely Monsieur Legrand, who had a beard and played the guitar. Gloriosa decided that Veronica should go ask Monsieur Legrand if he wouldn't mind giving his pupils a few magazines: "You Tutsi girls know how to handle Whites, and for once it won't be to bad-mouth the Republic." Monsieur Legrand seemed flattered by Veronica's request, and the following day he brought a pile of periodicals to class: issues of *Paris Match* and *Salut les copains*. "If you want more," he added, "just drop by and ask me." Some of the girls were convinced his invitation was meant specifically for them.

The girls flicked feverishly through the magazines. Lengthy negotiations ensued to decide the sharing and cutting out of photos. Johnny Hallyday, the Beatles, and Claude François were keenly fought over. As for the female stars, Françoise Hardy and her guitar seemed too sad, but Tina Turner and Miriam Makeba caught the girls' fancy because of their color, but Nana Mouskouri had the most success thanks to her glasses. Everyone wanted Brigitte Bardot's picture, but there weren't enough to go around. Gloriosa divvied them up among her favorites. Only a handful of girls, out of either caution or actual devotion, insisted on the Pope's portrait and some views of Lourdes, Saint Peter's in Rome, or the Sacré-Cœur in Paris.

When Mother Superior proceeded to inspect the "rooms," she couldn't hold back a *"Mon Dieu!"* of stupor, indignation, and anger.

"Just look at that!" she said to Father Herménégilde, who was standing beside her. "We thought we had protected our girls from the evils of the world, and the world has come crashing through our doors. But I can guess who gave them these horrors, and I'll tell him quite bluntly what I think about this."

"Satan," the chaplain replied, "takes every available guise. I fear our Christian Rwanda may be under serious threat."

Mother Superior severely reprimanded the girls and grounded them for the two following Sundays, except of course for those who had hung up a portrait of the Pope. She ordered the girls to tear down the indecent images and hand them in to Father Herménégilde. However, in order to demonstrate a certain liberalism, she exempted the photos of Adamo and Nana Mouskouri. The chaplain, it was noticed, conspicuously tore up the photos of the crooners but spared those of Brigitte Bardot and endeavored to furtively slip a few into his cassock pockets.

Mother Superior and Father Herménégilde apparently paid no attention to Godelive's alcove. Yet her schoolmates were most intrigued by her decorative display. Apart from the obligatory icons of the Holy Virgin and the President, there was only one other image: a full-length portrait of the King and Queen of the Belgians, Baudouin and Fabiola. We also noticed that the royal portrait was not an illustration cut out of a magazine, but an actual photograph. When Godelive was asked why she'd chosen such a photo and how she'd obtained it, she got all mysterious, simply replying that she couldn't say anything, that all would be revealed soon. Exasperated at not knowing, Gloriosa tried to force open Godelive's suitcase while she was cleaning the chapel with a few other girls. But the padlocks withstood her attempts.

A few days later, Mother Superior gathered all the pupils and teachers in the large study room. She appeared quite moved as she stepped onto the stage. She cast an unusually maternal gaze over the pupils: "My girls," she declared, "we are about to experience a momentous event, a historic event, I'm not afraid to say. Our lycée, the lycée of Our Lady of the Nile, will have the remarkable honor of welcoming the Queen of the Belgians, Queen Fabiola. For King Baudouin and his wife are making an official visit to Rwanda. While the President and the King discuss politics and development, the Queen will visit the First Lady's Orphanage in Kigali, but she is also keen to recognize and encourage the Rwandan government's female advancement policy, of which our lycée is the best example. You are familiar with the generosity and piety of Queen Fabiola. She will therefore visit our lycée. We must extend a welcome that will show her the image of today's Rwanda: a peaceful, Christian Rwanda. She will be accompanied by the Minister of Female Advancement, perhaps Madame the First Lady, too, we don't know yet. She'll stay for a day, perhaps, or a half day, I have yet to receive the definitive schedule. In any case, we have a month to prepare for this extraordinary event. The lesson load will be lightened if necessary. I am counting on all you girls, and on you, the teachers, to contribute wholeheartedly to the success of this day, which shall remain forever engraved in our memories."

The joyful commotion that swept over the lycée during preparations for the royal visit delighted all the pupils. It was a constant whirl of comings and goings, yelling and hubbub, the bustle of the lycée hands as they repainted the corridors, classrooms, refectory, and chapel. The desks were removed from the large study room, and the walls were lined with wraparound fabric bearing images of the President and the King of the Belgians. Classes would be brusquely interrupted when Father Auxile came to get the choristers for a rehearsal, and then the Kinyarwanda teacher would dash in to choose the dancers. Nearly every day, a delegation would arrive from the capital to give instructions, ensure that preparations were advancing properly, and decide on security measures. The Education Minister dispatched his Principal Private Secretary; the Archbishop, one of his Vicar Generals; and the Belgian Ambassador, his First Attaché. The President's Head of Protocol came in person and held long discussions with Mother Superior and the mayor, who never left the lycée during this time but rushed breathlessly along the corridors and up and down the stairs from one visitor to another, mopping his brow, in an attempt to outdo Mother Superior and her protocols. The pupils would rush to the windows whenever an unannounced

Land Rover or military vehicle pulled up, and as the passengers climbed out of the official cars, there was always one girl who recognized a brother, an uncle, a cousin, a neighbor, or a friend. Without waiting for permission, and ignoring the teacher's feeble threats, they'd leave class to go greet him.

The lycée was a hive of unusual activity. To showcase the progress of female emancipation, and despite Mother Superior's reticence, it was decided to shorten the skirts of the girls' uniforms, on the orders of the Minister of Female Advancement. And the same minister sent a consignment of white shirts to replace the old yellow ones. They were practically transparent, which Father Herménégilde seemed to appreciate, despite the reticence he displayed before Mother Superior. A whole afternoon was devoted to fittings and to patches on the bolero jackets bearing the colors of Rwanda and Belgium – Belgian colors on the right, Rwandan on the left over the heart. The tenth-grade girls plaited basketwork pieces as gifts for the Queen; on them they embroidered in red and black fibers: LONG LIVE THE QUEEN, LONG LIVE THE PRESIDENT, LONG LIVE BELGIAN-RWANDAN FRIENDSHIP. The songs composed by Brother Auxile were censored by the mayor, and particularly Gloriosa, the watchful eye of the Party. She considered heavy praise of kings and queens unbefitting to a Republic, in a country only recently freed from the tyranny of the Bami and the entire aristocracy. It was suggested to the composer that he might celebrate the farmer's hoe and the peaceful development of the country, which had been returned to the common people thanks to the wisdom of its President – and with the assistance of Belgium, of course, and, if he insisted, the manifest protection of Imana and the Blessed Virgin. Brother Auxile did his very best, but the girls refused point-blank to learn "La Brabançonne," which he suggested they sing after the Rwandan song.

The population of Nyaminombe was mustered to welcome the Queen. Obviously, she wouldn't have time to visit the town itself, located three kilometers from the lycée, but all the inhabitants would form a guard of honor at the roadside waving little Rwandan and Belgian flags that had yet to be delivered. The crowd would cheer on the procession with shouts of "Hurrah, Fabiola! Hurrah, the President!" The word "queen," *umwami-kazi*, had been forbidden, for fear it might provoke some outdated nostalgia among some of the people. The *imiganda*, community workers, devoted themselves to filling in the ruts in the track. Eucalyptus branches were planted on either side of the track, since banana trees, which usually decorate the verges of roads along which official processions pass, struggle to grow at this altitude. A squad of soldiers set up camp close to the lycée and made numerous patrols. It was hoped that the Queen wouldn't express the wish to visit the source of the Nile (which wasn't on the schedule, in any case) for there was neither the time nor the resources to restore the damage inflicted on the statue by the bad weather.

Godelive's mysterious behavior continued. She followed the preparations for the visit with a knowing look, getting involved as little as possible and not answering any questions. Which irritated her classmates greatly. Keenly aware of the arrival of any vehicle at the lycée, she would leap up at every slammed car door. It was noticed that she'd packed all her belongings in her suitcase as if readying herself to leave. A week before the big day, Godelive was summoned to Mother Superior's office. The whole twelfth-grade class waited for her outside and then walked her back to her "room." She sat down on her bed, and after a long silence, seeing that her classmates weren't going to leave her alone, she finally spoke:

"Listen, I want to say farewell, I'm leaving, probably for a long time."

"Where are you going?"

"Belgium. I'm leaving with the Queen."

A stunned murmur spread among her audience.

"You're leaving with the Queen?"

"It's a secret. I'm going to tell you, but you're not to repeat a word. To anyone. Especially not the other classes. Swear it."

They promised her with utmost solemnity to remain silent.

"You know that Baudouin and Fabiola don't have children. They can't have any. I don't know if it's his or her fault. It's sad not to have kids, even more so for a king and queen. They're desperate. So the President thought that since they were coming to Rwanda, at his invitation, the most beautiful gift to offer them would be the gift of a child. You know very well it's the done thing in Rwanda. A family with no children isn't a family. They can't be left to that sorry fate. It's the very worst! So if there's a brother, a relative, or a neighbor with lots of children, then they must give them one. Otherwise, it means you despise that family, that you wish them ill. If you give up one of your children, it means they join a new family of course, but it's still your kid. You've saved a family and they'll always be grateful and respect you. That's what our President wants to do: he's giving up his daughter for the sake of Rwanda."

"And you're the one he's giving to the King of the Belgians? At your age! A big fatty like you! With your kind of grades! Can you see yourself as Fabiola's daughter?!"

"No, not me, he's giving one of his own daughters, Merciana, the youngest. She's nine and very light skinned, looks like her mother. She could almost pass for a white girl."

"So where does that leave you, then?"

"Me, I'm accompanying Merciana to Belgium. She needs someone to speak Kinyarwanda with so she's not too homesick, someone to cook her bananas or cassava when she gets a craving."

"Ah! You'll be her servant! Now it makes sense!"

"You all claim to be intelligent, but you know nothing. Every queen, every princess has her retainers, even in Rwanda in the olden days. They choose daughters of good families, of noble birth. They're called ladies-in-waiting. And it's a great honor to be a queen or princess's lady-in-waiting."

"But why did the President choose you?"

"My father keeps out of politics. He's a banker, as you all know. He's rich. He knows the President from way back. They were together at the Legion of Mary. He's trusted. The President told him: 'I feel reassured that one of your daughters, educated in Rwanda's best lycée, will be there to look out for my little Merciana. I'm doing this for Rwanda. By giving up my child, I'm saving Rwanda from poverty: the whites will be obliged to help us in return. We'll be a part of their family. It's more than a blood pact. Merciana will have two fathers, myself and King Baudouin, both of us linked by this shared child.' So my father didn't hesitate: I was chosen to accompany the President's daughter. After all, I was born in Belgium, and even if I can't remember it much, maybe I'm still a bit Belgian, so that's handy for adapting. Now leave me be, I've got to finish my packing."

The whole class immediately gathered in the library to discuss Godelive's revelations. So that no one might eavesdrop on the debate, they decided to discreetly lock themselves in the archives room. Goretti started off by saying that she didn't believe a word of what Godelive had said, that she was spinning tales. If the President was really giving up his child, how could he have chosen the ugliest and stupidest girl in the lycée to accompany her? Unless her father had paid for it or had made who knows what kind of promise. Gloriosa couldn't contain her indignation:

"You're insulting our President again. Things could end badly for you. Godelive said it, he's giving away his daughter to save our country. Merciana might not become queen, but she'll be a princess in Belgium. They'll marry her to a prince. The Belgians will be obliged to help us. How shameful it would be for them if the country of one of their princesses remained so poor. And Godelive is a true Rwandan, make no mistake, you can't measure that with grades, even less with beauty. She'll make a fine representative of the majority people."

"But if Fabiola's infertile," said Modesta, "why doesn't Baudouin take another wife? Kings can do that, because they absolutely must produce a successor."

"Baudouin's a very devout Catholic, he can't get divorced."

"One can always sort it out with the Pope. It's possible for kings. They're not ordinary folk. They pay, give kickbacks, and the Pope ends up annulling the marriage."

"Listen," Immaculée said, "I've going to tell you something: it's not Fabiola who's sterile, it's Baudouin who's impotent."

"Oh! And how would you know! Shame on you! If your mother could hear you!"

"I overheard my father say so. He often tells his friends. I heard him tell them when I was serving the Primus in the living room.

How they laughed! My father was in Kinshasa the day Congo became independent – it was still Léopoldville back then. I don't know if he saw it all or just heard the story, but here's what he said.

"King Baudouin arrived from the airport. He was standing in an open-top car, a huge American one like you see in the movies. So Baudouin was standing up, very tall and straight, not moving, like a statue. He was wearing a fine uniform, all white with a large kepi, and at his side was a saber, with gold trim, the King's saber. Kasavubu looked tiny. There were huge crowds on the boulevard and tons of police. Whites. Then someone stepped out of the crowd. It was a young, well-dressed man, wearing a suit and tie. He'd managed to get through the police lines, no one knows how, and was running after the King's car, which was driving really slowly. And, bam! All of a sudden, he snatched the saber; he stole the King's saber and brandished it above his head with both hands, so everyone could see he'd grabbed the saber belonging to the King of the Belgians. The car kept on driving. The King was still standing, motionless, not moving, as if nothing had happened, as if he hadn't noticed anything. It was like he was under a spell. Soon after, they caught a man with the King's saber. But everyone said it wasn't him who'd stolen it. The real thief was Mahungu, not a person, a spirit, an *umuzimu*, a demon, as Mother Superior would say. But whether Mahungu was a man, a spirit, or someone possessed by Mahungu's spirit, he was a great wizard, he poisoned the King's saber, he put some *dawa* on it. The saber was returned to Baudouin, and Baudouin became impotent. They tried everything to cure him. He consulted all the doctors in Europe and America, but the *dawa* were stronger. The white doctors couldn't do a thing. They even brought witch doctors to Brussels, from Buha in Tanzania, but I think my father was exaggerating. What's certain is that Baudouin will never have children. There, that's my father's story."

The whole class nodded approvingly at Immaculée's tale. Goretti summarized the general feeling:

"Yes, one must always be wary. There are always poisoners looking to make you sterile. I know some. Don't get too close to Fabiola, she must be poisoned too, and it could be contagious."

Over the next few days, the question was whether a presidential car would come to fetch Godelive or whether she would leave with the Queen following her visit. Godelive stopped speaking to anyone and gave a haughty smile to anyone who addressed her. Goretti remained convinced it was all nothing but boasting and lies. Gloriosa hadn't received any instructions from the Party, so she maintained a cautious reserve while noting that for the sake of Rwanda's best interests, they could have chosen someone more "political" to advise the rather young Merciana. Godelive would only allow Immaculée to visit her "room." Immaculée was considered throughout the lycée to be the arbiter of elegance, and was renowned for her knowledge of white women's beauty secrets.

According to what she told the rest of the class, Godelive asked her about makeup and hairstyles: she had noticed Madame de Decker's red nails and wanted to know all about nail polish and what was best for toenails and wasn't there also a polish for lips? And perfume, not the *amarachi* you could buy from the Pakistani's, but the real thing, the kind the white girls sprayed all over themselves, that came from Paris, what was it called? But above all: the skin-lightening products that were bound to be more effective than the tubes of Venus de Milo on sale at the market. In the magazines Monsieur Legrand had given them, she'd seen black women, American no doubt, who were almost white and had long, smooth, glossy black hair, and there were even some – Godelive wondered how – who'd gone blond.

Godelive was very worried. What would she look like among all these women who were white, blond, and perfumed? Immaculée's tales had the class in stitches, but two days before the Queen's visit, a huge black car arrived quite discreetly at dawn to collect Godelive. The lycée girls rushed in their nighties to look but only glimpsed the Mercedes driving out of the gates, with Godelive waving grandly through the rear window. Some said she was bidding them farewell, others that it was just to taunt them.

That very same day also brought great disappointment. The breathless mayor arrived to inform Mother Superior of the latest instructions the President's office had just telephoned through.

Mother Superior called together the teachers and all the staff to update them on the new arrangements. They would fill the pupils in later. Queen Fabiola's timetable was overloaded. In addition to the First Lady's Orphanage, she was to make a donation to the Gatagara Care Center for Handicapped Children and visit the Benebikira Sisters. Of course the lycée of Our Lady of the Nile was still on her schedule, but she could only spend an hour there. She didn't want to disrupt the pupils' timetable in any way, but she was intent on dropping in on a lesson for at least a few minutes to encourage the pupils and applaud the government's efforts to promote female education. They would therefore have to trim the welcome speeches, cut most of Brother Auxile's songs, and shorten the dances. Instead of convening in the large study room, they would welcome the Queen in the yard, weather permitting, or else in the entrance hall. It was agreed that the Queen would sit in on Sister Lydwine's geography class – for no more than ten minutes, the mayor instructed. The topic would be agriculture in Rwanda. There'd be a rehearsal in the afternoon, where they'd try to anticipate Fabiola's possible questions and prepare answers. Just before the sovereign's departure, the seniors would give her presents, and Brother Auxile's choir would sing the national anthem and, if time allowed, a few of the songs.

The Belgian professors protested: they had been promised a personal introduction to their Queen and a few minutes' conversation with her. They were told they could stand in the corridor outside the classrooms, and when Fabiola walked by they'd be able to greet her, and she'd probably address a few words to each teacher. The French teachers said they didn't feel particularly involved, but they'd gladly take a few photos as souvenirs. The mayor strictly forbade them to do so.

On the following day, the eve of the royal visit, things grew even more frantic. State security agents arrived, flanked by five white men in dark suits, definitely Belgians. They seemed to be in a hurry, walking so fast the mayor struggled to keep up. They had a meeting with Mother Superior in her office, inquired about the pupils' state of mind, consulted the list of teaching staff, and asked for details of the young French teachers. They questioned the mayor about the atmosphere in his district, and he assured them that things were extremely calm, that the people were in excellent spirits, that they were eagerly looking forward to the event, and that the Queen could count on a warm welcome, since he had been organizing and supervising all the preparations personally every day, from dawn till dusk, and sometimes a good deal of the night, too, over the course of the past month. But the whites, who are strangers to politeness, interrupted him and requested that he get to the point. He did manage, however, to advise them to watch the enclosures of a few Tutsi, and the Rwandan security agents nodded in approval. The police officers searched every inch of the lycée. Sister Bursar even had to show them her pantry, which no one had the right to enter except for her. While they rummaged behind the stacked cans of corned beef and jam, she jangled her bunch of keys in protest. The police officers then gave their instructions to the mayor and Mother Superior. Two of them, a Belgian and a Rwandan, remained at the lycée. They were installed in the guest bungalow.

The security agents' jeep had barely departed when a battered old minibus pulled up in the yard. Three whites wearing shorts, khaki canvas jackets, and bush hats piled out. They were followed by a black man in a bright red shirt and tie. The black man, who turned out to be a journalist from Radio Rwanda, asked to see Mother Superior. He produced a permit to take photographs, issued by the Ministry of Information, and introduced his companions as veteran reporters working for a Belgian daily and a French weekly. They wanted to do a report on the lycée of Our Lady of the Nile, which they said was renowned in Belgium and elsewhere as a pioneering school, a model of female advancement in central Africa. They'd take some photographs, interview some teachers and, if possible, some pupils, and naturally Mother Superior herself. Flattered, though a little anxious, Mother Superior asked them to be as discreet as possible, and dispatched Father Herménégilde as their guide. The journalists returned to their minibus and came back laden with cameras and tape recorders.

Father Herménégilde was quite shocked at the journalists'

curiosity, or rather their indiscretion. The whites wanted to see and record everything. Not only did they photograph the chapel, and the classrooms (Sister Lydwine was warned in time and raced through the lesson she had rehearsed for the Queen), but they insisted on viewing the dormitories, and the seniors' decorated alcoves. They prodded the beds, asked where the showers were, and even entered the kitchens, where they peeked inside the stew pots and went as far as tasting the beans Sister Kizito was preparing. They seemed fairly uninterested in Father Herménégilde's comments and pronouncements vaunting the government's titanic efforts and tremendous success in promoting girls' education, and preferred to ask a series of incongruous, inappropriate, and impertinent questions such as: Did they complain about the food? Didn't they feel too isolated? What did they do on their outings? Did they have boyfriends? What did they think of family planning? Was it their parents who'd be choosing their future husbands? Were they Hutu or Tutsi? How many Hutu and how many Tutsi were there at the lycée? Father Herménégilde motioned them to stay silent, but some of the girls, proud to be speaking into a microphone, got entangled in lengthy answers before finally asking: "Am I going to be on the radio?"

The dancers had to be assembled, since they really wanted to film them. The journalists relished the sight of these young women (all seniors) lined up in the gym in their sports gear. Veronica was an irresistible magnet to every camera. The journalists asked her to step onto the stage on her own to pose, first facing them, then in profile. "Fabulous, just fabulous! She could go on the cover!" A furious Gloriosa asked them why they were only interested in Veronica. They burst out laughing and said: "Okay, we'll take your photo too."

Just when they were preparing to get back in their vehicle, Father Herménégilde reminded them they were due to interview Mother Superior. "Out of time," they said. "We've already got all we need. Please thank the Reverend Mother. We'd like to go up to the source of the Nile. Is there anyone to guide us?" Outraged at their poor manners, Father Herménégilde took his revenge with a rambling explanation of how it was impossible since the track had been swept away by a landslide. "Plus," he added, "it's starting to rain, so you'd better get going if you want to avoid getting bogged down on your way back to the capital." The radio journalist and the driver firmly agreed with Father Herménégilde's advice, and the minibus set off, much to the chaplain's great relief.

They waited for the Queen. A long time. On every hill, the local Party chiefs had tried to mobilize all the inhabitants who were fit and able. Many objected. Especially the women. There was always a field of peas or millet that needed weeding, it couldn't wait, and then there was the desperately sick newborn who wouldn't tolerate being strapped to its mother's back for a whole day in the sun or rain. At last, enough folk were roused to garnish the verges of the track for two kilometers. Little Belgian and Rwandan flags were handed out to the children from the primary school close to Nyaminombe. The monitor showed them how to wave the flags and made them practice one last time the song he'd written to welcome the Queen: "Sing as if it were the President," he advised them.

The lycée was seething with excitement. The pupils, some of whom hadn't slept a wink, had gotten up long before the alarm bell and the groaning gates. There was swapping and squabbling over mirrors, combs, and tubes of Venus de Milo cream. There was endless disentangling of hair and envying of those who were fortunate enough to have had theirs straightened. Every girl wondered what they could do to get noticed by the Queen or, perhaps more importantly, the Minister accompanying her. But how, since they all wore identical uniforms? It was out of the question to wave at her or wink – impossible! The girls practiced smiles of enthusiasm and admiration. Some were counting on their light complexion and their smooth hair, but most relied on chance: maybe the Queen would stop in front of her and say something. And then she would never forget her. But that would take a miracle, and only Our Lady of the Nile could perform that.

For breakfast, Sister Bursar had opened a few of the large tins of jam usually reserved for the pilgrimage picnic or the Monsignor's visit. Then, alas, the girls had to return to their classrooms, since the Queen wanted to experience the lycée as if it were a normal day. Sister Lydwine repeated her geography lesson, without apparently getting bored of it, and ensured that the pupils answered the anticipated questions as spontaneously and naturally as possible. The other teachers quickly gave up on their lessons, since the pupils rushed to the windows as soon as they thought they heard the sound of the long awaited-motorcade. The Belgian teachers sat stiffly on their chairs, for fear of creasing their suits or getting chalk dust on them. The chosen singers and dancers waited in the gym, ready to take up their places in the yard at Brother Auxile's signal. The two police officers paced the corridors. The mayor raced back and forth between the track and the lycée. Father Herménégilde stood on the chapel steps rehearsing his welcome speech in a loud voice, accompanied by expansive gestures. Mother Superior was everywhere: she tried to reestablish some kind of order in the classrooms; she sent one of the French teachers, who'd appeared wearing an open-necked shirt, off to find a tie; she rearranged the beds in the dormitories; she summoned the lycée hands to wipe down the refectory tables once again and mop the showers; she discovered imaginary spiderwebs in every nook and cranny; she ran a rigorous finger along the tops of the books in the library, revealing a thin line of dust; she reminded Sister Kizito of the statutory size of the fried cassava . . .

The Queen was due at half past nine. At ten o'clock, the rain arrived. The clouds, which until then had held fast to the peaks up on the ridgeline, now rolled down the slopes to enshroud the lycée. Many of those waiting beside the track took advantage of this to sneak away. Then the fog spread into ephemeral filaments, but the heavy motionless clouds began to pour forth their cataracts of rain.

Just before ten thirty, Sister Gertrude ran down the corridor where all the classrooms were, shouting: "She's here! She's here!" The pupils, who had eventually returned to their seats upon Mother Superior's incontrovertible orders, all rushed to the windows at once. Through the rain-lashed panes, they saw two military jeeps with their hoods down, flanking the gates, then four Range Rovers covered in mud pulling up by the four steps leading to the hallway entrance. The passengers got out – the girls counted a dozen at least: as many men as women, as many blacks as whites. Two of them ran toward the vehicle parked nearest to the steps, unfurled huge umbrellas, and opened the car door. The Queen! – it could only be the Queen – and the Minister! – of course it was the Minister – stepped out and took shelter under the umbrellas, but it was impossible to distinguish their faces beneath the hoods of their rain capes. Mother Superior, Father Herménégilde, and the mayor, who were waiting on the highest step, bowed respectfully, and the Queen, the Minister, and their retinue dived quickly into the hallway without taking the time to acknowledge them.

The choristers and dancers, who'd been packed into the hallway because of the rain, recounted the scene to their schoolmates. Mother Superior addressed a word of welcome to the illustrious guests whose visit honored the lycée of Our Lady of the Nile lost in the mountains, then Father Herménégilde launched into the speech he had been correcting and editing right up to the last minute, but the Queen, at a discreet sign from one of her retinue, who never took his eye off his watch, made an adroitly delivered compliment interrupting the chaplain, whose eloquent stream seemed never-ending. The Queen, whose cape had been removed as soon as she entered, and who was now wearing an enormous hat, declared that she was happy and proud to be visiting the lycée of Our Lady of the Nile, which was training the country's future female elite in the spirit of Christianity and democracy. She had wanted to personally encourage the efforts of the pupils, the teachers, and the government. The Minister emphasized that the President, supported by the majority people, was working tirelessly for the country's development, and that this wouldn't be feasible without the cooperation of women, whose education, according to Christian morals and democratic principles, was one of his priorities. The blinding flashes of the two photographers in the Queen's retinue made the mayor leap out of his skin, and for a moment he thought there had been an attack. The man who never took his eye off his watch whispered to Mother Superior, who immediately invited the Queen and the Minister to continue their tour and visit the pupils and teachers in their classrooms, which she had expressly wished to do. The choristers complained that they'd rehearsed four songs with Brother Auxile and had only sung one, and even that song they sang while everyone was climbing the stairs, and they weren't even sure the Queen and Madame the Minister had heard it.

In the end, the Queen insisted on visiting all the classes. In each room, the teachers introduced themselves to the Queen, who gave a few words in reply and then expressed her congratulations and encouragement to the pupils. Her face seemed frozen in a fixed smile, except when she glanced briefly at the man with the watch. In Monsieur de Decker's class, there was some surprise at the reverence of his wife, who had accompanied her spouse to greet the sovereign. Fabiola lingered a few extra minutes in Sister Lydwine's class, as planned, allowed the teacher to ask her three questions, then, satisfied with the answers, asked the pupils what they wanted to be: nurses? social workers? midwives? To avoid disappointing her, the girls she had questioned chose, somewhat randomly, one of the three suggested professions. The man with the watch showed signs of impatience. The Queen, the Minister, and her retinue quickly made their way back to the entrance hall, where the seniors, who'd been brought downstairs while Fabiola was with Sister Lydwine, were waiting to hand her their gifts. Gloriosa and Goretti gave her the basketry and the embroidered place mats. She admired them, then handed the gifts to a lady in her retinue, heartily thanked the two pupils, asked their names, and kissed them on both cheeks. Then, flanked by Gloriosa and Goretti, the Queen spoke, declaring that she would retain an unforgettable memory of her visit, far too short for her liking, to the lycée of Our Lady of the Nile, how inspired she felt by all she'd just seen, and that they could always count on her to support the efforts being made by this beautiful country to promote female education and advancement. After saying good-bye to Mother Superior, Father Herménégilde, and the mayor, Queen Fabiola and the Minister returned, under the protection of the umbrellas, to the muddy Range Rover, while the rest of the retinue made a frantic dash for the other vehicles.

With the two military jeeps in the lead, the motorcade exited the gates, drove down the track, and disappeared behind the curtain of rain.

Queen Fabiola's visit nourished the girls' conversations for a long time to come. They regretted it had been such a brief visit, and that the fabulous program they'd spent so long so carefully preparing hadn't been able to take place as planned: the choristers and dancers were the most sour. Why was the Queen in such a rush? It seemed quite shocking. Do queens always walk that fast? Or all self-respecting women? It was clear evidence of the bad manners of white people. Veronica gave the example of the *bamikazi* of olden times, who knew how to move with dignified slowness, as if counting their every step, no one would have dreamed of asking them to hurry up, like that man with the watch seemed to be doing: time was for the *bamikazi* to decide. Gloriosa immediately replied that those queens were Tutsi, meaning lazybones who'd never lifted a hoe, parasites feeding on the labor of the poor. And that those weren't good manners for true Rwandan women.

Modesta remarked that with all the bracelets and anklets they wore, the *bamikazi* couldn't walk without being supported.

The discussion centered mainly on Fabiola's beauty. Most of them found her extremely beautiful, more beautiful than Madame de Decker, and white, whiter even than all the white women in the capital. Indeed, everything about her was white: she wore a white skirt, a white jacket a bit like a man's, white shoes that remained pristine – they wondered how she managed that. Some regretted that she hadn't worn a long dress with a train, a real queen's dress, like in their history book, like Cinderella's dress. Immaculée sententiously explained that the Queen was wearing a suit, and that that was how the women dressed over there, in Europe.

"She's no more beautiful than Queen Gicanda," Veronica couldn't help remarking.

"Your former queen!" Gloriosa burst out. "Her so-called beauty didn't do her much good. I don't foresee a great future for her, locked up in her Butare villa. And you Tutsi, you always think you're the most beautiful in the world, but beauty's switched sides now. Your supposed beauty will bring you misfortune."

And then there was the hat. The mystery of the hat. An enormous hat, white too, with pink silk bows, feathers, and flowers, a real garden, the Garden of Eden, as Father Herménégilde would have said. How did it manage to stay in place beneath the hood that protected Fabiola from the rain? Did she put it on under the umbrella before she entered the hall? That was the mystery. However she managed it, they were all agreed, it was a real queen's hat, better than a crown. Never had anything like it been seen in Rwanda. Only a queen could bear such a monument on her head.

They waited impatiently for news of Godelive. Had the King and Queen taken the President's daughter with them? Had they really adopted her as their own daughter? And had Godelive, the lady-in-waiting, accompanied them on the plane? They asked Sister Gertrude, who listened to the radio, whether she'd heard anything. Nothing was said on the radio. They sent letters to everyone they knew in the capital, particularly their girlfriends. They pieced together all the fragments of the story. What did turn out to be true was that the President really had intended to offer the Belgian royal couple one of his daughters. He'd taken pity on the childless King, and had willingly offered up one of his daughters to preserve the lineage. He hoped that this way, the Belgians would always be on the side of the majority people, as they had been at Rwanda's independence. He was joining the family: for the honor of their shared child, they wouldn't let him down. But the King and Queen hadn't grasped the matter. There are some things that whites will never understand. The Belgians had replied that of course the President's daughter could study in Belgium. That went without saying. But when it came to the gift of a child, they feigned not to hear, or to understand. The President's daughter stayed put, and so did Godelive.

"I was right," said Goretti. "Nothing but tall tales. Godelive is so stupid she ended up believing her own lies."

"We'll see what she has to say for herself when she gets back," the others ventured.

Godelive never returned to the lycée. She felt too humiliated to face the mocking of her schoolmates. But she did go to Belgium. Her father found her a chic boarding school. It was rumored that Mother Superior had something to do with that.

The Virgin's Nose

"Modesta," said Gloriosa, "have you ever taken a good look at the Virgin's face?"

"Which one?"

"Our Lady of the Nile, the statue."

"Yes, and? Sure, it's not like the other Marys. It's black. The whites put black makeup on her. Probably to please us Rwandans, but her son in the chapel, well, he remained white."

"But did you notice her nose? It's a straight little nose, a Tutsi nose."

"They took a white Virgin, painted her black, and kept that white nose."

"Yes, but now she's black, it's a Tutsi nose."

"You know, back then, whites and missionaries were on the

Tutsi side. So a black Virgin with a Tutsi nose was a good thing for them."

"Yes, but I don't want a Holy Virgin with a Tutsi nose. I no longer want to pray before a statue with a Tutsi nose."

"What can you do! You think Mother Superior or Monsignor would really change the statue if you asked them to? Unless you talk to your dad . . ."

"Of course I'll talk to my dad . . . In fact, he said they plan to de-Tutsify schools and government. It's already started in Kigali and at Butare University. You and me, we'll begin by de-Tutsifying the Holy Virgin. I'm going to correct her nose, and there'll be some girls who'll understand the warning."

"You want to break the statue's nose! When they find out it's you who did it, you'll probably get expelled."

"Don't be so sure, I'll explain to everyone why I had to do it: it's a political gesture, so they'll more likely congratulate me, and then there's my dad . . ."

"So, how are you going to do it?"

"It's not difficult: we smash the statue's nose and stick a new nose on. We'll go to the Batwa one Sunday, there are some in Kanazi. We'll get some clay, nicely prepared and mixed, the kind they make pots with, and we'll mold Mary a new nose."

"And when will you stick this new nose on?"

"We'll go at night, the day before the pilgrimage, so the next morning everyone will see Our Lady of the Nile with a new nose.

A true Rwandan's nose, the nose of the majority people. Everyone will appreciate it. Even Mother Superior. No need to explain it to her. Or rather yes, I'll explain it to them. I know a few who'll lower their heads, trying to hide their small noses. You'll be first, Modesta, with your mother's nose. But you'll help me because you're my friend."

"I'm scared, Gloriosa. You'll still get into trouble, and I certainly will too if I help you."

"No, you won't, we're militants, I'm telling you. What we're going to do is a militant act, and what with my dad, nobody will dare say a thing. They'll be obliged to change the statue and replace it with another one, a real Rwandan lady with a majority nose. You'll see, the Party will congratulate us. We'll be women politicians. One day we'll become ministers."

"You definitely, but me, I doubt it."

Gloriosa's plan bothered Modesta. She hoped her friend would stop thinking about it, that she'd give up on it soon. The pilgrimage was a month away, by then Gloriosa would have probably forgotten about the whole thing. What she'd said was just a joke, idle chatter to pass the time, because life is so monotonous at the lycée of Our Lady of the Nile that you get some strange ideas sometimes. There are girls who imagine that a white teacher has fallen in love with them, that he'll whisk them off, steal them away, just because he looks at no one else in class, so they'll leave with him in a Sabena plane; others say the Virgin talks to them at night and they write down everything she says in a notebook; some girls believe themselves to be queens from olden times, nobody can touch them, so precious, so fragile, always on the verge of fainting; others say they're going to die because they've been poisoned, poisoned for being too beautiful, more beautiful than all the rest, the jealous girls are after them with all kinds of evil spells, and they can't eat a thing because there's poison everywhere. These are bad ideas that whirl and clatter inside girls' heads, sometimes they remain there, sometimes they vanish. Modesta hoped Gloriosa's bad idea had disappeared like so many others.

The following Sunday, after Mass, Gloriosa told Modesta:

"Hurry up, we're going to the spring. I want to check out the place and see how we can race up to the Virgin of the Nile's hut. We need to know exactly how we can climb up there."

"You still want to do what you told me?"

"Of course, more than ever, and I'm counting on you if you still want to be my friend."

"It scares me," sighed Modesta. "I don't have a father like yours . . . but I'll help you since you say I'm your friend."

It was raining. As they walked along the track, Gloriosa and Modesta passed a few women on the way back from Mass, carrying their little benches on their heads.

"We really live in the clouds," said Modesta.

"I like this rain," said Gloriosa. "I wanted this rain and I didn't need Nyamirongi to make her come. There'll be no one going to pray to Our Lady of the Nile, even those who wanted to ask her for good grades, they won't venture up there."

They scrambled down the steep path to the spring, twisting their ankles in the gullies and grabbing on to shrubs to avoid slipping. They stopped at the edge of the basin where the Nile pooled before flowing on toward its river destiny. The statue of Mary seemed to tower out of reach beneath its sheet-metal shelter, which had been jammed – goodness knows how – between two huge rocks. Despite this protection, the rainy seasons had taken their toll on the statue. Her black face was marbled with white streaks, and her clasped hands and bare feet were speckled with patches of the same color.

"It's Our Lady of the Zebras," hooted Gloriosa. "See, she needs repainting, or rather changing, and that's really such a Tutsi nose, even if it's an albino Tutsi nose."

"Shut up. Don't say stuff like that, it'll bring us bad luck."

They climbed the scree slope, maneuvering round the huge rocks, all smooth and gleaming. In the crevice between them, four poles supported a platform made of planks, covered in moss and lichen, on which the Virgin's nook had been erected.

"You see," said Modesta, "it's too high. We'd need a ladder."

"You'll be the ladder. Take me on your shoulders and I'll hoist myself up by grabbing on to the planks while you hold me steady and push. We'll get there."

"Gloriosa, you're crazy!"

"Do what I say, and don't argue, if you still want to be my friend."

Modesta crouched at the foot of the platform. Gloriosa swung a leg over and settled on her shoulders.

"Go on, stand up."

"I can't, you're too heavy. And with your big butt in the way, I can't see."

"Grab on to the post."

Modesta gripped hold of the post, slowly lifting Gloriosa, who encouraged her: "Come on, keep going, we're almost there!"

"That's it," said Gloriosa. "I've got my elbows on the planks. Watch out, I'm pulling myself up, hold steady, I'm there."

Gloriosa managed to slip into the narrow passage between the rock and the sheet metal. She stood up and Modesta saw her disappear into the shelter.

"That's it, I'm touching her. I'm taller than her. See how easy it'll be, a good knock on the nose, and done!"

Gloriosa ran back between the side of the shelter and the rock.

"Watch out," she cried. "I'm going to jump, catch me!"

Gloriosa jumped and fell on top of Modesta, dragging them both to the ground.

"Look at the shape we're in," said Modesta, getting up. "My skirt's all muddy and torn, look right here, and my legs are all scraped up. What on earth will we tell the monitor?"

"We'll say we slipped on the way to pray to Our Lady of the

Nile. They'll feel sorry for us and praise our piety. Or instead we'll say it was bandits who attacked us and tried to rape us, but we escaped. I prefer the second version, we're courageous girls who were attacked by the Inyenzi, there's still some of them in these mountains . . ."

"You know very well there are no Inyenzi left, the Tutsi are traders in Bujumbura and Kampala now."

"My father says we must repeat, again and again, that the Inyenzi are still there, that they're always ready to return, that some do still get out and are among us, that the Tutsi who stayed behind eagerly await them, and perhaps even half-Tutsi like you. My father says we must never forget to frighten people."

Gloriosa figured that to make their tale sound credible when telling the monitor, it was better to wait until dusk before returning to the lycée. They took shelter in the abandoned shepherd's hut farther down the path at Remera. They stretched out on a bed made of layers of thick grass that seemed to have been recently replenished. "See," said Gloriosa, "the hut is used, even if the bed's a bit firm for the things people come here to do. I'll eventually find out who meets here." She stretched out on the bed: "Come lie next to me and lift your dress. You know what needs to be done to prepare for marriage, it's what our mothers always did."

"My poor girls, whatever happened to you?" cried Sister Gertrude when she saw Gloriosa's and Modesta's torn, muddy clothes.

"We were attacked," said Gloriosa, her voice breaking with emotion, "men with dark cloth disguising their faces, I don't know how many, but they pounced, I'm sure they wanted to rape us, probably even kill us, but we fought back, we picked up stones, we screamed, they heard a Toyota coming and got scared, they fled . . . But I know who they are, I heard what they were saying, it was the Inyenzi, there's still some of them around, hiding in the mountains, my father said so, they come from Burundi, they're always ready to attack us whenever they can, and they've got accomplices: the Tutsi here. We must warn Mother Superior."

The two *lycéennes* were shown into Mother Superior's office. Again, Gloriosa recounted the tale of the assault, but in this new version, the details were much worse: the number of Inyenzi kept on growing, and now it was the lycée they were preparing to storm, they wanted to rape all the pupils, and torture them horribly and kill them, the nuns wouldn't be spared either, not even the whites. Modesta kept quiet: she made herself whimper and cry as Gloriosa had instructed. "Hurry," insisted Gloriosa, "there's not a moment to lose, we're all in danger, the Inyenzi are close by, they're everywhere."

Mother Superior made the necessary decisions. She summoned Father Herménégilde, Sister Gertrude, and Sister Bursar for a war council. She sent Brother Auxile to Nyaminombe in his truck, and he returned with the mayor and the two gendarmes.

She assembled the girls in the chapel, and Father Herménégilde made them sing hymns, interspersed with dozens of rosaries, without telling them why. Sister Bursar distributed kitchen knives to the lycée hands, carefully jotting down the number in her notebook, then took command of the brigade posted at the school gates. Night had fallen. Sister Bursar decided to hand out all the biscuits she'd been saving for the next pilgrimage. In the chapel, despite Father Herménégilde's stubborn insistence on litany upon litany of hymns and rosaries, the spreading rumors finally got the better of him. It was whispered that the President had been assassinated, that the Inyenzi had crossed the lake, that the Russians had given them monstrous weapons, that they were going to kill everyone, even the young women, after raping them first . . . Many were in tears, some asked the chaplain to take their confession, others hoped, though they didn't know why or how, that they'd escape the massacre, if not the raping.

The sound of Brother Auxile's truck was heard. The suspicious guards, fearing that the truck had fallen into an ambush, opened the gates slowly, in spite of the driver's impatient honking. With some relief, they saw that Brother Auxile had brought not just the mayor and the two gendarmes with their rifles, but also twenty militants armed with machetes.

The war council met again in Mother Superior's office: present were Mother Superior, the mayor, Sister Bursar, and Father Herménégilde, who'd left the girls under Sister Gertrude's watchful eye. As both victim and witness, Gloriosa was invited to attend and recount the attack for the mayor's benefit: the supposed Inyenzi were now more numerous and violent than ever, and Gloriosa lifted her dress to show them all the scratch marks covering her thighs. Modesta, still silent though now sobbing for real, was led to the infirmary so that Sister Angélique could look after her. The mayor declared that he'd been able to contact the Prefect, who then alerted the army base. The colonel was going to immediately send fifty soldiers under Lieutenant Gakuba's command. Meanwhile, they placed militants at the strategic points and dispatched a patrol of militants to the shopping district, led by a gendarme. Mother Superior gave the girls permission to return to their dorms and get into bed, but with their clothes on.

They all waited. The night was particularly dark and the mountain was still. The patrol returned from the village. A few dogs stirred, and the mixture of plaintive and furious barking took a while to quell. Soon after midnight two trucks rolled up, packed with soldiers. They immediately took up their positions around the lycée. The young lieutenant in command conferred with the mayor and Mother Superior in her large office. Gloriosa retold her tale, this time adding that she thought she had recognized the voice of one of those who'd attacked them, she wasn't entirely sure, but it could well have been Jean Bizimana, the son of Gatera, the Tutsi who had a stall at the market. The lieutenant said that the Tutsi were never far from the Inyenzi, and that there was no doubt that the bandits, who had come from abroad, were now hiding with them. He would send out patrols to search their compounds, taking the militants as their guides. Jean Bizimana would be arrested immediately. "When it comes to the Inyenzi, there's never a moment to lose," said the lieutenant.

The operations ordered by the lieutenant were promptly carried out. The patrol chiefs returned an hour later to report to him in the presence of Mother Superior, the mayor, and Gloriosa, who had refused to go and lie down in the guest room they had offered her, even though it was the finest one, Monsignor's room. Jean Bizimana had been arrested without offering any resistance, amid the screams and tears of his parents, his brothers, and his sisters. The soldiers had interrogated him with the intensity needed to make him give up his accomplices. He admitted nothing. They were going to send him to the huge prison in the north of the country. "There's little chance we'll see him hanging around my district again," said the mayor, laughing.

The soldiers had ransacked the few enclosures still inhabited by Tutsi. They'd conscientiously ripped open granaries, smashed jars, questioned every occupant, even the children. In vain. The Inyenzi had fled without a word. "So," said the lieutenant, "two brave young ladies succeeded in putting them to flight. Still, it's a shame we couldn't catch a few. But it was a good operation: the Tutsi need constant reminding that here in Rwanda they're merely cockroaches, Inyenzi."

Gloriosa stayed in Monsignor's room for a few weeks – until the pilgrimage, as she'd requested. They couldn't refuse anything to a girl who had shown so much courage, and whom Father Herménégilde had compared to Joan of Arc in one of his sermons. The two lycée girls' exploits, Gloriosa's especially, were celebrated in even the highest echelons of the Party. "Two heroic lycée girls deflect band of dangerous criminals come to sow chaos in our country," ran the newspaper headline. Gloriosa had become the heroine who had saved the lycée, perhaps even the entire country. The nuns and the teachers took every opportunity to compliment her: the gaggle of schoolmates that clustered around her grew considerably larger, although some avoided chatting with her for too long, for fear of committing some sort of faux pas. Only Goretti kept her distance, allowing herself to covertly express to those of her friends who remained loyal some doubt as to the authenticity of Gloriosa's exploits.

Modesta hoped that Gloriosa would renounce her intention to mutilate the statue of Our Lady of the Nile, for fear of compromising her newfound fame, but one day in Sister Lydwine's class, Gloriosa whispered to her, "Don't forget, Sunday, we're off to the Batwa."

The Batwa village comprised a dozen disheveled little huts in the middle of a sparse banana grove. On a well-flattened stretch of ground, a large blackened circle marked the site of the fire where the clay pots were baked a few days before market. All around stood piles of potsherds, like low, crumbling pyramids.

Seeing the two girls approach, a swarm of squealing, naked children fled, their balloon-bloated stomachs streaked clay white. The village felt empty, strangely silent. They walked along the paths leading to the huts and finally came across a woman molding a pot. From a base made out of a broken pot, upon which sat a pile of clay, she brought forth – coil upon coil – the smooth, rounded belly of a stew pot. The potter was so absorbed in her task that when Gloriosa and Modesta drew near, she didn't look up. They gently coughed to get her attention. After a while, without ceasing her work or looking at them, the woman mumbled: "If you're here to buy a pot, they're not ready yet. They're drying. Come by the market, I'm always there. Then you can buy as many pots as you want."

One by one, the kids who'd run off at the sight of the girls came out of their hiding places, drew closer, surrounded them, pressing tight, trying to touch them. Adults, men with beards, and yakking women slowly mixed in with the children. "Tell them to step back, I don't want them to touch me," said Gloriosa to the potter, clutching the folds of her skirt. "Get back," said the potter, as an old man with a pointy white beard emerged from a hut and pushed away the most brazen with his staff. He came and sat down by the potter. Gloriosa explained what she wanted: a wad of clay, which one of the teachers at the lycée had asked for. The potter and the old man didn't seem to understand. Gloriosa repeated her request.

"So you want to be a potter," said the old man, bursting with laughter. "You want to do what we Batwa do. Are you a Mutwa? You're quite big for a Mutwa!"

"Give me one of those clay sausages," Gloriosa insisted. "I'll pay you the price of a whole pot, a jug, a large jug."

Conferring in low voices, the woman and the old man gave it some thought, now and again glancing up at Gloriosa and Modesta with mocking grins.

"Two jugs," said the potter at last, "two large beer jugs, that's my price, and you'll get your sausage. Twenty francs, that'll be twenty francs."

Gloriosa handed the potter a twenty-franc note, which the woman immediately crumpled into a ball and thrust into the knot of her wraparound. She called over one of the children, who went off to pick her a tuft of grass. This she wove into a kind of net in which she wrapped one of the clay coils with which she made her pottery.

"Here," she said, "but don't tell anyone what's in here. Otherwise, they'll say you've become a Mutwa."

Gloriosa and Modesta hurried away as fast as they could, with a crowd of joyous, shouting, singing, dancing villagers following them as far as the track.

When they were finally alone again, Gloriosa opened the grass envelope and gazed at the clay coil for a long while.

"Look," she said, "there's enough here to correct the nose of every Virgin in Rwanda!"

"It's all here in this bag," said Gloriosa, "everything we need for tonight."

Gloriosa opened the bag and Modesta saw that it contained a hammer, a file, and a flashlight.

"Where'd that come from?"

"Butici, the mechanic guy borrowed it for me from Brother Auxile's workshop."

"Did you give him money?"

"No need. He knows who I am. He was more than happy to help me out."

"And how are we going to get out of the lycée at night?"

"You'll come get me from my guest room, since they put you back in the dorm. They won't refuse you that. Anyway, I'll ask them to let you come. It won't be hard to jump the wall behind the Bungalow, I've checked where there's a gap."

"So you still want to do what you said?"

"More than ever! Now that I'm a heroine, and you too, they'll say it's another one of our exploits, and believe me, it will be."

"You know very well it's all based on your lies."

"It's not lies, it's politics."

"We'll set off when everyone's asleep," said Gloriosa. They waited for the lycée to sink into slumber. First there was the hubbub of the girls as they returned to their dorms, followed by the murmur of the last prayer they recited before climbing into bed. The ringing bell and the creaking gates signaled the start of curfew. Half an hour later, the purring of the generator ceased. The watchmen, spear or machete in hand, made their last round, then wrapped up in their blankets at the foot of the gate and fell asleep, despite instructions to the contrary. No lamp shone at Mother Superior's office window. "It's time," said Gloriosa. "Let's go."

They scaled the wall at the end of the garden without any difficulty, and enveloped themselves in their wraparounds. "Here, you carry my bag," Gloriosa told Modesta. "I'll go in front." They paused at the edge of the track. The familiar landmarks had vanished into the night. It was as if the mountains had swelled with a thick mass of darkness that filled even the vertiginous drop, at the bottom of which the lake could be glimpsed.

"We'll get lost," said Modesta, "switch on the flashlight."

"It's too dangerous. There could still be some army patrols or militants roaming around. I really scared them with my Inyenzi."

They managed to feel their way along the track and reached the parking lot overlooking the spring. The trail leading down to the spring had been evened out and graveled, in readiness for the pilgrimage no doubt. Gloriosa switched on the flashlight. They rounded the huge rocks, and to their surprise found a ladder leaning against the platform. "See," said Gloriosa, "we're in luck, it's a sign that we're carrying out a patriotic act: the gardeners who came to clean the shelter and decorate it with flowers have left their ladder."

Gloriosa climbed onto the platform and, clutching the hammer, the file, the coil of clay, and the flashlight Modesta passed to her, wriggled around in front of the statue and kicked over the vases of flowers, which fell into the spring water pooling in the basin. Balancing precariously on the edge of the platform, Gloriosa dealt the Virgin's nose such a blow with the hammer that the head of the statue shattered to pieces. She clambered down from the platform and turned to Modesta, who was shivering with cold and worry.

"I've broken Mary's head, it'll be impossible to fix her nose. But at least now they'll be forced to replace the statue."

"And what will happen to us? What a hideous sin!" Modesta whined. "If they ever realize it was us who did that . . ."

"Modesta, you're always worrying. I already know what I'm going to do."

At dawn, the lycée was filled with joyous effervescence. The great day had arrived, pilgrimage day! The girls took out their new uniforms, which had had their first outing for the Queen's visit, but the patch with the Belgian colors had been gently removed from the bolero jacket and replaced with one provided by Father Herménégilde, embroidered with the intertwined colors of Jesus and Mary.

Everyone gathered in the yard, in front of the chapel, each class lined up behind the banner that the girls had been embroidering in sewing class since the start of the year. Father Herménégilde blessed them and Brother Auxile handed out stenciled sheets of his latest hymns. Sister Bursar counted out cans of sardines, corned beef, Kraft cheese, and jam, which she packed into large baskets that the lycée hands then hoisted onto their heads. Silence fell when Mother Superior appeared on the chapel steps flanked by the mayor, the two gendarmes – with guns on their shoulders – and all the teachers. She made a short speech reminding them of the history of Our Lady of the Nile, urging everyone to conduct themselves most piously, and, turning to the mayor, she declared that this year they'd be making a special plea to the Black Virgin to bring peace and harmony to the thousand hills of this beautiful country.

The procession moved off, walked through the gates guarded by the militants, followed the track along the ridgeline, then proceeded down the path and arranged themselves, class by class, on the slope facing the spring. Suddenly, there was a shriek of horror: the Virgin had lost her head, or rather what was left of it resembled cracked pottery. The Madonna's face had been smashed, and the shards lay scattered on the platform. Flowers floated on the water of the basin, which was threatening to overflow, since one of the vases had blocked the drainage channel.

"Sacrilege! Sacrilege!" shouted Mother Superior.

"It's the devil's work," cried Father Herménégilde in turn, making frantic gestures of blessing, as if he were performing an exorcism.

"Sabotage," muttered the mayor, dashing behind the rocks, his arm soon appearing above the decapitated statue holding a black ball.

"A grenade!" yelled a white teacher, before running up the path, his colleagues close behind, as they climbed the slope with newfound agility.

One of the gendarmes raised his rifle to his shoulder and fired toward the bottom of the hollow, into the spreading ferns, beneath which flowed the stream.

Panic spread among the girls. They jostled and trampled each other, stampeding up the path, oblivious to the orders, pleas, and entreaties of Mother Superior entangled in her long dress, of Father Herménégilde gathering his cassock, of the panting mayor, who brandished the dirty black ball crying: "It's nothing, it's nothing, it's just clay!" The lycée hands had dropped the large baskets of provisions they'd been carrying, and the cans were now rolling down the hill, to the great despair of Sister Bursar, who'd quickly given up trying to run after them.

All the fugitives gathered in the lycée yard. Everyone caught their breath. "To the chapel," ordered Mother Superior, and when everyone had taken their place in the pews, she spoke:

"My girls, you witnessed this ghastly sacrilege. Impious hands – I don't wish to know whose – have violated the sweet face of Mary, our protector, Our Lady of the Nile. It befalls us to expiate this crime against God. We shall fast. Today we shall eat nothing but boiled beans. May God forgive the person or persons who committed such a sin."

That's when Gloriosa slipped out of her row of pews and walked up to the altar steps. She whispered in the ear of the mayor, who then went over to Mother Superior. They conferred quietly together for a long while. Finally, Mother Superior blurted out:

"Gloriosa has something to tell you."

Gloriosa rose to the highest step before the altar. She scanned her schoolmates, giving several of them a mocking or satisfied smile. As soon as she began to speak, her booming voice made everyone jump:

"My friends, it is not in my name that I ask to speak to you, it is in the name of the Party, the Party of the majority people, that I address these words to you. Our Reverend Mother Superior said she didn't wish to know who smashed the head of Our Lady of the Nile, but we are well aware that those who committed this crime are our eternal enemies, the executioners of our fathers and our grandfathers, the Inyenzi. They are communists and atheists, led by the devil. They want to burn down the churches, kill the priests and the nuns, and persecute all Christians, like they do in Russia. They've infiltrated everywhere. I'm even afraid that some of them are here, among us, in our lycée. But I am confident that Monsieur the Mayor and our armed forces will know how to get the job done. What I wanted to tell you is that we'll soon have a new statue of Our Lady of the Nile, and she'll be a real Rwandan woman, with the face of the majority people, a Hutu Virgin we'll be proud of. I shall write to my father. He knows a sculptor. Soon, we'll have an authentic statue of Our Lady of the Nile, a true likeness of Rwandan women, to whom we'll be able to pray without hesitation, and who will watch over our Rwanda. But as you know, our lycée is still full of parasites, impurities, and filth that render it unfit to receive Our True Lady of the Nile. We must get to work without delay. We must clean everything, down to the smallest recess. No one should be disgusted at such work, for it is the work of true militants. There, that's all I wanted to tell you. Now let us sing the national anthem."

All the girls clapped, the mayor launched into song, and everyone joined in as one:

> *Rwanda rwacu, Rwanda Gihugu Cyambyaye*
> *Ndakuratana ishyaka n'ubutwari*
> *lyo nibutse ibigwi wagize kugeza ubu,*
> *nshimira abarwanashyaka*
> *bazanye Repubulika idahinyuka*
> *Twese hamwe, twunge ubumwe dutere imbere ko . . .*

Rwanda, our Rwanda, who gave birth to us,
I celebrate you, oh you, courageous and heroic.
I remember the many trials you have experienced
And I pay homage to the militants,
Those who founded an unshakable Republic.
Together, in unison, let us forge ahead . . .

"You see," said Gloriosa to Modesta as she returned to her pew, "here, I'm already the minister."

School's Out

During the month following the attack against Our Lady of the Nile, lycée activities focused on preparing for the triumphant welcome reserved for the new and authentic Madonna of the River. The old statue was unceremoniously removed from her niche. Nobody knew quite what to do with her. To destroy her was perhaps dangerous, for they feared the vengeance of She who had been venerated for so long, and to whom so many prayers had been addressed. Draped beneath a tarpaulin, She was eventually consigned to the maisonette at the bottom of the garden housing the generator. For a long time, they suspected old Sister Kizito of dragging herself on her crutches – when she could – to go and pray before the One whom she'd seen erected above the spring with such solemnity and fervor.

Gloriosa was triumphant. With Father Herménégilde's militant blessing and steady assistance, she'd proclaimed herself President of the Committee for the Enthronement of Our Authentic Lady of the Nile. They occupied the library, which they'd turned into their headquarters, and which was now out of bounds except with their permission. The telephone, which until then had been reserved for Mother Superior's office, was now set up in the library. Gloriosa went to class only rarely now. With Father Herménégilde at her side, she would interrupt the other classes without hesitation, to make short speeches, in Kinyarwanda, phrased as slogans heavy with double meaning. She had managed a spectacular reconciliation with Goretti, welcoming her as a committee board member. But Goretti, while approving and encouraging Gloriosa's activism, had refused the post of vice president Gloriosa offered her, and displayed a cautious reserve in front of the other girls. Mother Superior hardly left her office now, and when she did, pretended not to notice the disorder that reigned in her establishment. When Father Herménégilde came to see her, out of a respect for hierarchy that barely disguised a hint of insolence, to update her on the committee's activities, Mother Superior merely replied:

"Very well, Father, you know what you're doing, Rwanda is an independent country, independent . . . but don't forget, we're responsible for a lycée of young women, they're only young women . . ."

And then she plunged her nose back into the inventories she'd asked Sister Bursar to provide so she could check them, on the pretext of planning the start of the next school year.

Gloriosa and Father Herménégilde went on a mission to Kigali and Butare for a few days. A giant Mercedes, provided by Gloriosa's father, came to collect them. Upon their return, they hastily called a meeting of the committee, informed Mother Superior, and announced a general assembly of pupils and teachers in the large study hall. Gloriosa let Father Herménégilde speak first. He revealed that, with the support of the highest echelons of government and the Party, the enthronement of Our New and Authentic Lady of the Nile would be the occasion for a gathering of the elite of the Militant Rwandan Youth, the JMR, who at this very moment were continuing their parents' glorious social revolution throughout the country. High school and university students would drive up to Nyaminombe in minibuses. Around fifty were expected, students selected from among the best of the militant youth. Tents supplied by the army would be erected on the open land above the spring, for there was clearly no question of housing boys in the lycée, so close to the young women. The ceremony would be both religious and patriotic in nature. He finished his speech in Kinyarwanda, proclaiming that the Rwandan youth would swear an oath to Our Lady of the Nile, who henceforth stood for true Rwandan women. He told them to always remember the centuries of servitude they had endured at the hands of arrogant invaders, to continue to defend the gains of the social revolution, to tirelessly fight those who remained the implacable enemies of the majority people both outside and within Rwanda's borders. Then Gloriosa, still speaking in Kinyarwanda, added that it wouldn't be long before the lycée of Our Lady of the Nile followed the example of those brave militants who rose up in schools and in local government to rid the country of the Inyenzi's accomplices. The girls of the lycée of Our Lady of the Nile, Rwanda's female elite, would prove worthy of their parents' courage, and she, Nyiramasuka, would be worthy of her name, of that they could be sure.

Everyone in the hall applauded. Only Monsieur Legrand dared utter a feeble objection:

"But how will we complete the school program, what with this big celebration coming up? Isn't there a risk of being refused certification and losing a whole year?"

Father Herménégilde answered him with extreme courtesy, saying that the foreign teachers – friends – had nothing to worry about, for none of it concerned them anyway. The lycée of Our Lady of the Nile, which was considered the best in the country, had nothing to fear, and would be crowned with the national certification of its end-of-year exam, just as it was every year.

"It's coming, Virginia, you do realize that? Don't think we'll escape it just because we're in a lycée for the privileged. On the contrary. We're their biggest mistake. And they won't be slow to correct it. Gloriosa has engineered the whole thing: that business of the phantom Inyenzi, the attack on the statue, the Hutu's new Madonna. It's all in place. All that's missing is the JMR gathering. And they won't come singing hymns to Mary, they'll come with fat truncheons, with clubs, maybe even machetes, to honor Their Lady of the Nile. I suppose the new girls have properly understood what's going to happen to us. But if there are any still clinging to their illusions because they can't get over having been accepted into the lycée for future ministers' wives, then they must be warned. Discreetly. It's too dangerous for us all to get together. Imagine the plot: a Tutsi meeting! And when the time comes for us to flee, we'll each have to go our own way. Some will get caught, but some will manage to escape, I hope."

"Listen," said Virginia, "I'm not leaving the lycée without my diploma. Give up so close to the diploma? Never. If you knew how much this means to my mother, the dreams she's built upon that piece of paper. When I think of all those girls who were just as smart as us, maybe smarter, and were excluded by the famous quota. They had to resign themselves to simply being farmers, poor women farmers, all their lives. It's partly for them I want to get this diploma, even if it probably won't be very useful in Rwanda. After all, it's not the first time we've been threatened, it's our daily burden. Let's wait to get that diploma, and if we have to leave, I'll figure out a way."

"I'm not so sure. You know, they've started to hunt Tutsi bureaucrats and students across the whole country. Soon it'll be the turn of the lycée of Our Lady of the Nile, why would we escape it? The purge will end with a bang at the lycée of the female elite. You know what awaits us. Have you forgotten what we've already suffered and what they're promising every day will happen to us? In 1959, half my family fled to Burundi as refugees. In 1963, three of my uncles were killed, though my father escaped – in Kigali, they didn't do as much killing as they'd have liked to because of the people from the United Nations – but he was sent to prison with loads of others, he was beaten to a pulp, and when they let him go – because the President wanted to show the whites just how peace loving he was – they made him pay a colossal fine, his taxi and truck were impounded, and to top it all off, they made him sign a document confessing he was a spy and an Inyenzi accomplice. My father's frightened: that document is still with State Security. Because of that, now they might kill him."

"If they kill our parents, they'd better kill us too. You know what happened when we took refuge at the mission? There were many orphans, their mothers and fathers had just been massacred. Well, the Prefect came to say there were some Hutu families willing to adopt them, and he used such fancy words in front of the missionaries, like Christian charity and community spirit, that when my father repeats those words, they make him angry and my mother starts to cry. Anyway, they shared out the orphans: boys went to work the fields, and the young women, well, they were very popular, you can imagine why! When, as Gloriosa has promised, the JMR get here – and we know what for – there'll still be time for us to hide, and try to join our families, then cross over to Burundi."

"I'll go to Fontenaille's, he'll protect me, he won't let me fall into the hands of rapists and murderers. I'm his Isis, and anyway, nobody except you knows I go there."

"Are you really sure? No one followed you there? You didn't say anything to Modesta? I have doubts about her sometimes: why does she like talking to us Tutsi so much behind her great friend's back? Because she's half Tutsi or because she's spying on us? Why does she complicate her life so much, poor thing?"

"I don't know. It's hard to tell. Perhaps she's guessed something. She often asks me what I'm up to on Sundays, then laughs and makes allusions to that crazy old white guy who loves sketching beautiful Tutsi girls so much."

"Watch out. Even if her mother's Tutsi, you know what side she'll always be on."

"But, Virginia, if we really have to flee, how will we do it? The lycée is the only thing in Nyaminombe. It's surrounded on all sides. I bet the mayor, his police officers, and the militants are already watching it closely. And when the day comes, they'll put up roadblocks on the track. Even if you dress as an old peasant woman, it won't be in a Toyota that you'll leave Nyaminombe. Don't count on anyone inside the lycée. Mother Superior's already shut herself away in her office, so she can't see anything. The Belgian teachers will keep on teaching, unperturbed. Even though the French teachers have some affection for us, seemingly because of our physique, they'll obey the instructions from their embassy: no interference, no interference! When the killers fall upon us, some will say: it's always been like that in Africa, savages killing each other for reasons no one understands; and even if some lock themselves in their rooms to cry, their tears won't save them. But I have one hope, and that's Fontenaille. You know he sent my portraits off to Europe, I'm known over there. He keeps saying they're expecting me. He can't let me be killed right in front of him without doing anything. Come with me. You're his Queen Candace too. He must save his goddess and his queen."

"I won't be going to hide at your white's place. It's odd, but I'm not scared, it's like I'm sure I'll get out of it, as if someone, something, had promised me."

"Like who?"

"I don't know."

Virginia was counting down the days leading the Tutsi girls toward a destiny she considered inevitable. There was no doubt that the scenario envisaged by Father Herménégilde would play out, step by step. Yet she couldn't get rid of that certainty deep down inside her that somehow she'd escape it, and this troubled her. Meanwhile, Gloriosa had deemed herself absolute mistress of the lycée, and her sovereignty extended to the refectory. The table upon the stage, from where Sister Gertrude and the monitors would watch over meals, was empty now. Gloriosa declared she no longer wished to open her mouth in front of the Inyenzi. From now on, they would eat after the real Rwandans. They took great pains to leave them the quota of food that the majority people still conceded to the parasites. All the other tables followed her example. Gloriosa also decreed that no one should speak to the Tutsi-Inyenzi anymore, and that they must be prevented from talking among themselves. The true militants would always keep a watchful eye on them, and inform her of any suspicious word or deed. Virginia noticed, however, that Immaculée always managed to be the last one to get up from the table, discreetly leaving a good share of her portion.

Virginia could no longer sleep, nor did she want to. She listened for the slightest sound, anxiously waiting for the creaking gates, the rumbling engines and screeching tires that would announce the killers' violent arrival, to be followed by furious shouts, screams of protest, hobnailed boots hammering the stairs, the stampeding panic of flight . . .

Virginia hoped it would occur at night. She thought this would make it easier for her to shake off her pursuers in the lycée corridors, reach the garden by way of the staircase that led down to the kitchen, jump the wall, and run and run toward the mountain . . . But she had no idea what might happen after that. She couldn't picture it. But whatever the case, it had to be a moonless night.

Her head was filled with endless scenes of her escape, always the same, but one night she couldn't stay awake and had a dream that reinforced yet further her vague certainty of being spared that she just couldn't explain. She saw herself wandering the labyrinth of a vast enclosure, the kind they used to build for the kings of old. Beneath the bundles of bamboo that framed the entrance to a courtyard, stood a man, waiting for her; he was young, and very tall, with features that appeared, to her eyes, faultlessly beautiful. "Don't you recognize me?" he asked. "Even though you came to see me, don't you recognize Rubanga, the *umwiru*?" He handed her a huge pot of milk: "Go carry this to the Queen, she's waiting for it, she's waiting for you." Virginia continued on her way, between the high intertwined fencing, finally emerging in a vast yard where beautiful young women were dancing to the gentle rhythm of a song that reminded her of one of her mother's favorite lullabies. The Queen stepped out of the large hut, her face hidden by a veil of pearls. Virginia knelt before her, and offered up the pot of milk. The Queen drank with delightful slowness, then handed the pot to one of her retainers and spoke to Virginia: "You have served me well, Mutamuriza, you are my favorite. Here is your reward." Virginia saw two shepherds leading a pure white heifer toward her. "She's yours," said the Queen, "her name is Gatare, remember, Gatare."

Virginia was suddenly awakened by the creaking gate. It made her jump. The killers? The ringing of the wake-up bell reassured her. This new day was beginning like all the others. Her head was full of the memory of her dream. She took refuge in it, felt herself wrapped in an invisible protective force. She repeated the name of the cow from her dream like an incantation: "Gatare, Gatare." She would have liked to remain forever in that dream.

The new statue of Our Lady of the Nile arrived in a tarpaulin-covered van. She was immediately surrounded by a crowd of lycée girls. But they were disappointed. The statue was enclosed in a wooden crate, which the lycée hands heaved onto their shoulders, according to Father Herménégilde's anxious instructions, and carried into the chapel. The chaplain shut himself in with Gloriosa and forbade entry to anyone. They heard the hammering of the lycée hands as they dismantled the crate. "She's beautiful," said Gloriosa as she came out of the chapel, "very beautiful, really black, but no one must see her until the lycée's fit to welcome her, and Monsignor to bless her." The girls rushed inside the chapel anyway, but all they saw was a shapeless form in front of the altar, wrapped in a huge Rwandan flag.

Virginia looked for Veronica, but in vain. She wasn't in class, nor did she appear for refectory. The twelfth graders acted as if they hadn't noticed their classmate's disappearance. Only Gloriosa remarked – loud enough for Virginia to hear: "Don't worry, Veronica's not gone far, I know there are some among us who know where she is. I know too, and from a reliable source," she added, looking at Modesta. As everyone rushed upstairs to the dormitory, Modesta managed to whisper a few words to Virginia: "Whatever you do, don't go to that old white guy's place, find another way out, but above all don't go there."

All through the night, Virginia wondered how to warn Veronica. Seeing the statue arrive, Veronica must've gone to seek refuge at Fontenaille's, since that was her only plan. But it was no longer a secret at all, everyone knew her hiding place. Virginia squeezed back tears of rage and anguish so no one could say to her in the morning, laughing: "See, despite your pretty name, we've succeeded in drawing a few tears from you."

Despite the growing chaos that had engulfed the lycée, the teachers still held their classes as usual. The timetables, and the teachers' presence and punctuality, were the only regulations Mother Superior still managed to enforce, as long as she shut her eyes to the repeated absences of some of the pupils. One day in class, Monsieur Legrand asked for a pupil to go get the exercise books he'd collected for marking, and which he'd left in his pigeonhole in the staff room. Immaculée beat everyone else to it. When she returned, she handed out the exercise books. Upon opening hers, Virginia found a small square of paper. She read:

"When the JMR arrive, apparently it's tomorrow, don't flee with the others. Try to go up to the dorm, go to my room and wait for me there. Trust me, I'll explain. Destroy this note, swallow it if you must. Immaculée Mukagatare."

Virginia read and reread the small piece of paper she held in the palm of her hand. Immaculée's plan might be ingenious, but should she trust her? Immaculée wasn't really her friend. Of course she wasn't part of Gloriosa's gang. She appeared to laugh at politics, and particularly Gloriosa. All she seemed interested in were her looks. So why take so many risks to save a Tutsi? Hiding in Immaculée's room meant placing herself entirely in her hands. And what would she do then? But there was Immaculée's name, her true name, the one her father gave her, Mukagatare. Gatare, was that what her dream meant, Gatare, that which is white, that which is pure? Again, she felt in the grip of some invisible protective force. Yes, she'd follow the plan suggested to her by Immaculée, Mukagatare, what did she have to lose?

When it happened, it was pretty much as Virginia had predicted. Two minibuses sped through the gates and halted right in front of the steps at the main entrance. Young men – extremely young men – got out brandishing huge clubs. Immediately, the Tutsi girls rushed into the corridors in a desperate attempt to flee. The other pupils went in pursuit but were unable to catch them. Virginia spotted an empty classroom. She entered and hid under the teacher's desk. The horde of pursuers ran past shouting. When she was sure the corridor was deserted, Virginia couldn't help looking out of the window onto the yard. She saw Gloriosa giving her instructions to the man who seemed to be the leader of the militants. She had no trouble understanding the plan Gloriosa had hatched: the pupils were to hustle their Tutsi classmates into the garden, where the JMR gang and their clubs lay in wait. Virginia opened the door a crack. There was no one in the corridor. She tiptoed down it. In the empty classrooms, the Belgian teachers sat at their desks, clearly seeking the appropriate demeanor in such a situation. The French teachers huddled together, plunged in deep, animated discussion. As if protected by a halo of tranquility, Virginia went up the stairs to the dorm, without meeting anyone, and reached Immaculée's room. She made sure that in the event of danger, she could hide under the bed. She waited, attentive to the slightest sound. Shouts and screams came from behind the building, from the garden she thought, shuddering. Soon, she heard steps, and threw herself under the bed.

"Are you there?" asked Immaculée.

"Is that you? Immaculée, what will you do with me?"

"Now's not the time to explain. Listen to me. There's a wraparound for you on the bed, put it on. You're going to hide at Nyamirongi's, the rainmaker. I've arranged everything. I sent Kagabo to ask her. According to Kagabo, the rainmaker accepted without a fuss. Nobody will come looking for you there. I'll send

Kagabo when there's a car to take us, I'll take you in the trunk if I have to. Hurry up. Kagabo's waiting, you've nothing to fear from him, I've given him enough money, and anyway, witches don't like having anything to do with the authorities. I'll go ahead to warn you of any danger."

"At the market," Immaculée had said. "He's waiting for you at the market." By that time of the afternoon, the market had long finished. A few scrawny dogs were squabbling with crows and vultures over small piles of refuse. From behind a barricade of old, rusty metal drums, she heard a quiet: "*Yewe*, this way." She found Kagabo crouching by a bundle of dry wood. He looked her up and down somewhat derisively.

"Your wraparound's much too new to pass for a poor farmer, give me that."

He stood up, took the wraparound, roughly scrunched it up, and rubbed it about in the dust, and in the delta of fetid rivulets that streaked the ground.

"All right, that'll do, take off your shoes and come over here."

He took Virginia's face between his hands, reddened with earth, rubbed her cheeks, and gave her a piece of filthy cloth to cover her hair.

"So, now you look like a poor farmer. Take this bundle of sticks, put it on your head, and walk slowly, very slowly, like a real farm woman. There's nothing to be scared of, everyone's afraid, they don't understand what's going on, they don't dare go out, the traders have all closed shop. And remember, I'm here to protect you – it's not wise to approach a poisoner."

When Virginia entered the smoky hut, she saw only the shifting play of shadow and light caused by the leaping flames in the hearth. From the dark interior, by the foot of the woven-straw vault that the fire didn't reach, came a feeble voice:

"You're here, Mutamuriza, I've been waiting for you, come closer."

Virginia walked toward the back of the hut until she eventually discerned the silhouette of an old woman, wrapped and hooded in a brown blanket, from which emerged a wrinkled, lined face that brought to mind the monkeys who used to plunder her mother's maize field.

"Come closer, don't be scared, I knew you'd be coming, don't think it was Kagabo who told me you were on your way; I knew well before he did, and even before that girl who sent him to ask me to take you in. I know who's sending you to me, and it's for Her that I agreed to harbor you."

"How can I thank you, Nyamirongi? You've saved my life and I have nothing to give you in return. I left all I had at the lycée. But no doubt Kagabo gave you what my friend wanted to give you on my behalf."

"He brought it for me. But I didn't want it. I'm not doing this for your friend, so there's no reason for her to pay me. If I'm harboring the favorite of She who dwells on the side of Shadow, it's because She will grant me her favors too – that I know."

"Can you see into my dreams?"

"I saw a white heifer and She who gave it to you, but I didn't see them in a dream, I saw them when the spirits carried me to the other side of Shadow. You're the favorite of the Shadows, so be welcome at Nyamirongi's."

Virginia settled in with Nyamirongi. Each day she prepared her sorghum gruel. Nyamirongi seemed appreciative. Virginia noted that the granary behind the hut was well stocked. Nyamirongi must have no shortage of "clients." When night fell, she crouched by the fire, stretched out her right arm, pointed her forefinger with the very long nail to the four compass points, then withdrew it beneath her blanket, and simply nodded, muttering some words that Virginia wasn't able to grasp. A week passed. Virginia grew increasingly worried. What had happened at the lycée? What had become of Veronica? And all the other girls? Had any of them succeeded in escaping? She forced herself to believe they had. Had Immaculée forgotten about her, had someone informed on her? Hiding behind a rock, Virginia spent her days watching the slope that ran down to the lycée.

But one evening, Nyamirongi's arm, forefinger, and long nail began to shake and she had to use her left arm to pull it back. She looked at Virginia, eyes bright:

"The rain tells me she's leaving, making way for the dusty season, as she should. She also tells me that down there, in Rwanda, the season of men has changed. But she tells me, too, not to trust it: those who believe in quiet times, the lightning will catch them. They'll be struck, and they'll perish. You'll be leaving me soon. Tomorrow, I'll tell your fortune for you."

Nyamirongi woke Virginia before dawn, and threw a small log on the embers to revive the fire.

"Come, we must tell your fortune before daybreak. The spirits stop answering once the sun is up."

She reached for a large basket and plucked nine knucklebone jacks from a little bag made of fig tree bark.

"The sheep gave us his bones so we may divine destiny. You must never eat sheep."

She closed her eyes and tossed nine jacks into the basket. Opening her eyes, she contemplated the constellation formed by the jacks for a long time, without uttering a word.

"What do you see?" asked Virginia, a little worried.

"You'll leave Rwanda, and go very far away. You'll learn the whites' secrets. And you will have a son. You'll call him Ngaruka, 'I shall return.'"

"Look," said Kagabo, "your friend's waiting for you there, in the car."

The rear door of the Land Rover opened, and Virginia saw

Immaculée, who motioned her to get in: "Hurry up. We're heading back. No need to hide, but still, don't attract too much attention to yourself."

"I don't understand," said Virginia. "Tell me what's going on."

"Nyamirongi talks to the clouds but she doesn't have a radio. There's been a coup d'état. The army's taken over. The former President is under house arrest. As soon as they heard the news, the militants piled into their minibuses and sped off. It was Sister Gertrude, who always listens to the radio, who told us the news. Nobody knows where Gloriosa's dad is, perhaps he fled, or else he's in prison. Everyone turned against Gloriosa, and started cursing at her. She's the one who plotted everything: the troubles, the violence . . . Because of her, the Humanities diploma was in danger of not being certified. The whole school year would be lost. And all the fault of that ambitious girl whose father might now be in prison. Goretti made a long speech. She forced Gloriosa to listen to it: now it was the real Hutu who'd seized power to save the country, those who'd resisted all the colonizers, be it the Tutsi, the Germans, or the Belgians. Those who'd been contaminated by Tutsi ways would do well to start speaking real Kinyarwanda, the kind still used in the foothills of the volcanoes. Everyone was now able to understand Goretti without any difficulty, and some girls even tried to imitate the way she speaks. An army car came to fetch Gloriosa, nobody knows what's become of her. But I'm not too worried about her, with an ambition like hers, Gloriosa,

Nyiramasuka! She's still got a future in politics! We'll be seeing her again. She'll make her way. Then Mother Superior announced that the long vacation would start eight days early – the embassies had recalled their teachers to the capital, the lycée had to close, she had told parents to come get their daughters, and had hired minibuses for those who couldn't be picked up. Father Herménégilde said the enthronement of Our New Lady of the Nile was postponed to the start of the next school year, and that we'd use the occasion to celebrate national unity. Me, I managed to tell my dad, and he sent his driver. Hey, let's get going."

"And the other girls, at the lycée, what became of them? Did they escape? No! They killed them?"

"I don't think so. Not all of them, anyway. You know, apart from Gloriosa, there weren't that many who really felt like killing their classmates. Chasing them from the lycée, yes, they agreed with the idea there was no room for Tutsi girls. When I returned to the yard, Father Herménégilde was telling the militants things like this: 'Hound these Tutsi from the lycée, but there's no need to get your hands dirty. Catch a few, whack them a few times, that'll make them lose their taste for studying. They'll perish in the mountains, of hunger and cold, or be devoured by feral dogs and wild beasts. Those who survive and manage to cross the border will be forced to sell those bodies of theirs that they're so proud of, for the price of a tomato at the market. Shame is much worse than death. Let us leave them at God's mercy, for his judgment.' I figure many were able to escape, and find refuge in the missions, with some of those old white missionaries still nostalgic for the time when the Tutsi were their favorite followers; or else they were able to meet up with Tutsi priests driven from the parishes that had protected them: perhaps they succeeded in crossing the border together. Even the farmers, not all of them are prepared to kill young, educated women because of some school business that doesn't concern them. Now they're in Bujumbura, Bukavu, or elsewhere. I haven't heard of any deaths. If any of the lycée girls had been killed, Gloriosa wouldn't have missed the chance to brag about it. But Gloriosa really wanted to kill you and Veronica, she couldn't bear the thought of seeing you standing alongside her to receive your diplomas on the solemn graduation day."

"And Veronica, where's Veronica? What happened to Veronica?"

"I don't know. Don't ask me."

"Yes you do, tell me."

"I don't want to tell you."

"You have to. You owe me that."

"I'm ashamed to tell you, it scares me, now everyone scares me. I realize all human beings hide something terrifying within. Even my boyfriend, I don't want to see him anymore: he wrote to me saying how proud he was to have acted like a real militant, of having beat up some Tutsi in his college, he's not sure if he killed any, but he hopes that some will become invalids, with all the blows he gave them. I don't want to see him anymore. Do you still want to know what they did to Veronica? Well, I'll tell you, but don't cry in front of me, you are Mutamuriza, the one who we mustn't make weep. If you cry, it'll bring me bad luck.

"So, when the JMR were done with expelling the Tutsi, Gloriosa told them, 'There's two missing: I know where one is, but the other must be hiding in the lycée. She must be found, and I want you to do a proper job on her. I want to see her weep every tear in her body. Mutamuriza! They must take us students seriously!' The militants looked everywhere, they ransacked the entire lycée. You were far away by then, of course. Gloriosa was furious. She flung herself at Modesta, who as usual was following her like she was her dog. She started cursing at her: 'Dirty bitch, it's you who warned Virginia, telling her to run away. She was your friend, your true friend, you spied on me for her, I'm going to punish you like the parasite you are. You've stuck to me too long to be able to trick me. You clearly are your mother's daughter. You've only handed over half the Inyenzi. Well, I'm going to make sure you're cleansed of that Tutsi half of yours that betrayed me.' She called three militants. The men dragged Modesta into a classroom. We heard weeping, pleading, cries, and whimpering. It lasted a long time. Then we saw Modesta dragging herself to chapel, trying to cover up her bloodied body with her tattered uniform. Gloriosa was calling out to all the militants, saying to them: 'There's another Inyenzi, a real one, even more dangerous, thinks she's queen of the Tutsi! I know where she's taken refuge. Not that far away. At an old white guy's place. We really can't let her get away. The white guy's in cahoots with the Inyenzi. He's made his coffee plantation their hideout, a base to attack the majority people, he's recruited young Tutsi, training them like commandos. Meanwhile, he invokes the devil, while his Tutsi Veronica he's turned into his she-devil, and together they commit abominable acts, just like Queen Kanjogera, who, according to my father, killed four Hutu every morning to work up an appetite. She dances for the devil. We must be rid of these demons. Do it, quickly'.

"Twenty militants left in one of the minibuses, with a Nyaminombe militant acting as their guide. They returned at nightfall. They were really riled up, shouting, 'We got them! We got them!' Then they threw themselves upon the bottles of Primus. Gloriosa asked the leader to recount his exploits. He didn't need to be asked twice. He said that first they overran the villa. There was no one around. They smashed all the furniture. Then they went into the garden – that's when they saw the devil's chapel. They entered. Painted on the wall was a whole procession of stark naked Tutsi girls worshipping the great she-devil on the back wall – a real Tutsi wearing a hat with demon's horns. At her feet was a sort of throne, and on the throne the she-devil's horned hat. They heard some noise behind the chapel. They ran. The white guy and the Tutsi were trying to hide in the little bamboo wood.

The white guy had a rifle but didn't have time to use it. They all pounced on him and knocked him out. They grabbed Veronica. They took her to the chapel. The leader of the militants said she looked exactly like the she-devil painted on the wall. They undressed her, and forced her with blows from their sticks to dance stark naked before the idol that resembled her, then they tied her to the throne. They put the hat on her head. They spread her legs. I won't tell you what they did with their sticks, nor how they finished her off. Then they went and set fire to the enclosure that crazy white guy had had built on his estate. They didn't find the Inyenzi that Fontenaille had recruited, they'd long since fled, but they did slaughter the cows, and burn them too. The leader of the militants brandished the hat with the horns. He was still mad with rage. 'Here,' he shrieked, 'the Inyenzi queen's crown, the devil's hat, but it's all over for her now, she got the punishment she deserved, which will continue in Hell. I regret we didn't kill all the other girls, but I hope we'll track them down one day.'

"The following morning, the mayor went with his police officers and the militants to arrest Fontenaille and serve him his expulsion order. They found him hanged in his chapel. They claimed he killed himself. If it was the JMR who killed him, they didn't brag about it. Killing a white is always a delicate matter for the government. The girls who had listened to the leader of the militants were trembling, some were crying, yet still they had to applaud. 'You see,' said Gloriosa, 'the Tutsi god is Satan!' Personally, I don't believe all this devilry business, it's just more of Gloriosa's lies. It was horrible what they did to Veronica. Now I'm certain there's a monster lurking inside every human being: I don't know who awoke him in Rwanda. But tell me, what was Veronica doing at this Fontenaille's place? Were they shooting a movie? She'd always loved the movies so much . . . You must know, Virginia, you were her best friend, everyone knows she hid nothing from you."

"I don't know. Don't say another word, and don't ask me anything if you don't want me to cry."

They remained silent a long time. The track wound endlessly through narrow valleys, climbed hillsides covered with thick banana groves, followed ridges scattered with patches of eucalyptus, plunged back down into more valleys, ascended more slopes . . . Virginia struggled to squeeze back her tears and blot out the horrific images that assailed her, again and again.

"Immaculée, I owe you my life, but I still don't understand why you did all that for me. I'm a Tutsi, I wasn't really a friend of yours . . ."

"Well, I like a challenge. I think I was more attached to that motorbike which terrorized the streets of Kigali than to my boyfriend; I went to see the gorillas because I loathed Gloriosa; I wanted to save you both, you and Veronica, because the others wanted to kill you, and now I'm going to defy everyone, I'm off to be with the gorillas."

"You're going to live with the gorillas!"

"I found out that the white woman who wants to save the gorillas will be recruiting Rwandans to train them as assistants. I have all the qualifications: I'm Rwandan, an intellectual, I think I'm quite good-looking, and my father's a well-known businessman. I'll be good publicity for her: she'll be obliged to take me. But what do you intend to do? You're not going to abandon your diploma, are you? You know that the army declared that they took power to reestablish order. They want to calm down the same ones they stirred up. In any case, those folk got want they wanted: the Tutsi's positions. I'll ask my dad to intervene, if necessary. I understand why he so kindly drove me to Goretti's at Ruhengeri: it was to inform army headquarters they could count on his money. They can't refuse him a thing, and when it comes to his daughter, he refuses her nothing."

"I'm done with that diploma. I'm going home to my parents to bid them goodbye. And I'll leave for Burundi, Zaire, or Uganda, anywhere, wherever I can cross the border . . . I no longer want to stay in this country. Rwanda is the land of Death. You remember what they used to tell us in catechism: God roams the world, all day long, but every evening He returns home to Rwanda. Well, while God was traveling, Death took his place, and when He returned, She slammed the door in his face. Death established her reign over our poor Rwanda. She has a plan: she's determined to see it through to the end. I'll return when the sunshine of life beams over our Rwanda once more. I hope I'll see you there again."

"Of course we'll see each other again. Rendezvous at the gorillas'."

archipelago books

is a not-for-profit literary press devoted to
promoting cross-cultural exchange through innovative
classic and contemporary international literature
www.archipelagobooks.org